A Mortal Affect

A

NOVEL

by

VINCENT STANDLEY

A Mortal Affect
© 2011 Vincent Standley

ISBN: 978-0-9831633-4-3

Typeset by Ambivalent Design
Typeface: Adobe Jensen

Cover design by
Sandy Florian
Vincent Standley
& Derek White

Cover art sources:
Albertus Magnus from *Symbola Aurea Mensae*
by Michael Maier, 1617

Ad for the Edison Mimeograph Typewriter, 1895

Published by Calamari Press

calamaripress.com

For Sandy Florian and Michael Martone

Timeline

The Age of Nothing
0
First action of first mystery language
second action of first mystery language
creation of nine plates of gold
creation of the new rain

The Age of Existence
1,000,000,000,000,000 After Nothing
creation of the unexistent
creation of small waves & small authors

The Age of Imogravi
1,000,000,000,000,001 A.N.
Revelation of Imogravi
creation of flint
creation of specific builders
creation of lower surfaces
creation of the net of the impossible

The Age of Annihilation
1,000,000,000,000,002 A.N.
Relocation of Imogravi
Destruction of first universe

The Second Age of Nothing
1,000,000,000,000,003 A.N.
second first action of first mystery language
second second action of first mystery language
second creation of nine plates of gold
second creation of new rain

The Second Age of Existence
1,000,000,000,000,004 A.N.
second creation of the unexistent
second creation of small waves & small authors

The Second Age of Imogravi
1,000,000,000,000,005 A.N.
second revelation of imogravi
second creation of flint
second creation of specific builders
second creation of lower surfaces
second creation of the net of the impossible

The Age of Invisibility
1,000,300,000,000,005 A.N.
second relocation of imogravi
creation of kosmocratores
creation of tiny angels

The Age of Matter
1,000,300,001,000,005 A.N.
creation of animal kings
training of officials
smelting of teeth
building of imperial palace & admin district

The Age of Mortality
1,000,300,001,100,005 A.N.
creation of first root-race
creation of second root-race
creation of third root-race
creation of fourth root-race
creation of fifth root-race
creation of sixth root-race
creation of seventh root-race
creation of eighth root-race

The Age of History

1,000,300,001,100,107 A.N.
Ascendancy of Lineal Descendant
Convocation of Assembliers
Passing of Bar by Circle of Nine
Creation of Ninth Root-Race

The Age of Departure

1,000,300,001,100,207 A.N.
Creation of elemental beings
Implementation of valence retrofit
Departure of Kosmocratores

The Age of Tyranny

1,000,300,001,115, 050 A.N.
Reascendancy of exiled Lineal Descendant

The Age of Reform

1,000,300,001,120, 000 A.N.
Installation of Blue spires

The Age of Suicide

1,000,300,001,120,075 A.N.
Pseudo-Death of Lineal Descendant
Mortal marriage of Lineal Descendant

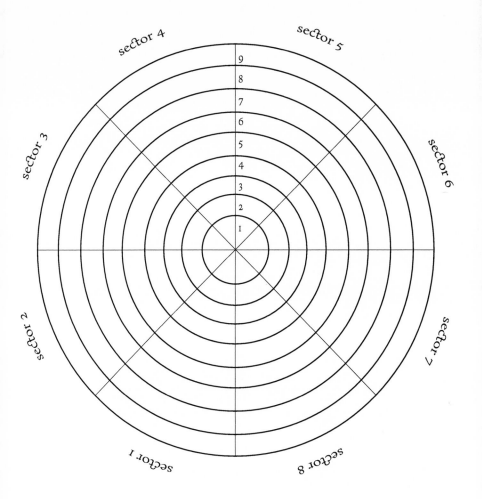

I
spires

i

ʙlue

Modular welfare blocs, each nearly as tall as the Grid wall itself, encircled the Outer Ninth and housed over forty million mortals. ʜɪɢʜ-ᴏᴄᴄᴜᴘᴀɴᴄʏ, ʟᴏᴡ-ᴍᴀɪɴᴛᴇɴᴀɴᴄᴇ: ᴛʜᴇ ꜰᴜᴛᴜʀᴇ ʟɪᴇs ᴀʜᴇᴀᴅ embossed on plaques in clear block letters were affixed to every outside entrance, tarnished but still legible after three millennia. The buildings had fared almost as well, with their graffiti and quarry mold. Then, one by one, they all turned blue. Not without warning—a flood of social workers implemented bloc meetings to inform Rooters about the change, its rationale from a planning perspective, and the nuts and bolts of volumetric display technology—and not all at once—one or two buildings from each district, until the Ninth Circle was lit up like a halo around the entire Creation Grid. The forever-gray and rectangular welfare housing became almost majestic: radiant blue spires, modeled, they were told, on the Palace of the Lineal Descendant.

Miles away, the immortals working in the neighboring Eighth thought the projections were a distracting annoyance but considered them preferable to the drab view of mortal squalor. For the tenants, blue saturated every surface and sliver of open space; it flickered with a static, nervous buzz, illuminating places once dark, strobing in sync with florescent lit interiors and street lights. People knew it simply as *the glare*, after a profile piece on the contemporary welfare apartment. The Rooter journalist wrote, "Inside the Blue Spires, light echoes off walls; it's a twenty-four hour glare."

Inside their apartments Rooters covered the windows with newspaper and flattened cardboard boxes. They replaced fluorescent lamps with hard-to-find incandescent bulbs, bartered for in the back rooms of distribution stations and meeting halls, traded with earplugs, ambient-sound cassettes, and spire-light lenses, mass-produced in the Bauble District promising *A natural light without strobing. Barter-back-guarantee.* Out-of-doors escape was even harder as they ventured past concrete porticos into a light that had replaced all other light. They described being cloaked in a blue aura that clung well past the siege of projectors and hissing transducers, seemingly extending just beyond each step. They went out when the sun was brightest and the blue was less intense. They wore yellow so the yellow appeared green, anything to reclaim the space that had been taken. These measures would have been mere gestures if so many claimable things hadn't already been claimed, if they weren't already living with discards and nonessentials to create distinction and consequence.

Drouth

Gale stood beside their bed. Since he'd been up, Dorthea had commandeered both blankets and was now wound-up clockwise like a bean twist.

"Morning Dear."

"It's not morning yet."

"But you look so delicious."

"Go eat another breakfast."

"*Kosmocration*, okay, grouchy wench."

"And coffee for me."

"Of course."

"Thank you."

The coffee percolated, and Gale put on slippers and left for the hallway. Beyond their seventh floor apartment the air was dank and blue. A swath of black and green mold grew inches deep across the concrete walls and ceiling, mucoid and glistening. Black spores speckled the floor and windowsills; they made the air appear impure. The mold patch would soon reach the apartment. *Cripes!* No maintenance crew had been their way since the collapse of the ninth floor fire escape. Standing water from upstairs made its way slowly downward, between concrete slabs, past iron rebar, staining the walls in a slow cascade of brown.

The mold is black and yellow not green...

Dorthea said that by design the corkboard created the illusion they had control over their environment. When she asked why he bothered, he had no explanation, only thinking it ironic that the housing blocs were masked to be something they weren't, while every Rooter masked their home to be something it could never be: a safe refuge. So he checked for notices and missives on the board. If there was something—and usually there wasn't—it was likely bad news—only underscoring the argument against his checking in the first place.

Last week Dorthea had said, "Look, so there are two possible scenarios, two likely scenarios. One, you go out and nothing's there, which by your own admission is usually what happens, and which we both agree is a waste of time. Or, two, there is something, but it's bad news; that is, in our experience anything on that board is probably bad news and if not bad news then annoying news, like cobblestones being moved from one side to the other or the Circle Nine arriving at 11:48 not 11:50, or whatever. We agree on this point, right?"

"Absolutely."

"When you persist in going out morning after morning, one can only wonder at some other motive. All I know is that when you open the door, the blue malignancy fills *our* apartment. And when you come back, you look like a walking hologram."

He trusted her and did not argue but chose not to alter his morning routine.

Facing the corkboard, he was rewarded by an envelope addressed to their apartment. General announcements were dispersed to everyone in the housing bloc, taped to doors, left in stacks at the downstairs entrance; a few might be tacked to the corkboard, usually Malking propaganda, amateurish and baffling. There might be an announcement for an upcoming inconvenience, as Dorthea's examples suggested, only less ridiculous and more banal. Formal-looking letters were usually subpoenas or official responses to complaints made by other tenants. Neither was common. A subpoena could mean anything. Each year a few tenants got carted off in prison baskets, some to be tortured, others to be returned the next day unharmed. Everyone came back. Execution had been dropped from the Malking list of dos. The tortured were replaced by hollow, wrecked versions of themselves, the least depressive becoming depressed, even suicidal. Those not tortured returned simply confused, unsure why they'd been summoned in the first place. Malkings functioned by procedure. A guilty verdict was always accompanied by a public writ stating the violation and the penalty mandated by law. Everybody knew a single penitentiary for forty million mortals meant a low rate of incarceration. Why be scared at all? Again, Gale had no answer. He just figured Rooters had started out that way.

He untacked the envelope and went back to the apartment. The address was handwritten not mimeographed. The envelope contained a single-page letter with the logo of the Bureau of Root-Race Affairs and Security: a row of silhouetted figures—evidently Malkings and Rooters in alternating sequence—holding hands. BRRAS: IN IT TOGETHER! arched over the figures in the rough semblance of a rainbow, all set in mimeograph blue.

Dorthea was upright in bed, a blanket pulled over her shoulders, revealing little more than her face. She yawned as Gale reentered reading the letter aloud.

"'Annual review at the Welfare Stadium. Mandatory attendance'. Blah, blah, blah."

"Enough. Move on. Edicts aren't the best morning fare."

"Okay, but check this out, there's a bit at the bottom: *And the world shall burn before the last cataclysm*. Handwritten too."

"..."

"A handwritten address is weird enough—"

5

"Right, but read that part again."

"It says, *And the world shall burn before the last cataclysm.* That's the part at the bottom."

"Show me."

He handed her the letter. She read it over then crumpled the paper and tossed it over the kitchen counter.

"Shit."

He retrieved the paper. "What is it?"

"This is bad."

"I think we've faced worse than this." He pulled back a corner of the cardboard window cover and held the paper up to a wash of blue light.

"Shut that please."

"Not until you tell me the secret message."

"Could you make food?"

"Anything to help build the suspense."

"I recognize I'm being a *Malking* pain in the ass."

She got out of bed, retaped the cardboard, and padded to the bathroom.

They ate hot bean grits with raisins as the ball of paper slowly uncurled on the table.

"I can't tell you anything very specific," she began. "I don't know why it was sent, what it means, or who sent it."

"Well, that clears things up."

"I can say with total certainty that it wasn't accidental and clearly shows someone has information they shouldn't."

"How's that?"

"It goes back to my parents."

"I think by now, we both know that's inescapable."

"You know me as Dorthea. I mean, I am Dorthea and have been called Dorthea since childhood."

"Glad to meet you Dorthea, my name is Gale." He proffered a hand.

"My birth name is Drouth."

"…"

"Not Dorthea…Drouth."

"That's unfortunate," said Gale. "Not a total train wreck, though, right?"

"Listen. Drouth is from the *Archaic Record*, so it would be sacrilege for a Rooter to have the name. By naming me Drouth, my father was making a distinction between our public and private life. He was saying there are two mes. The Drouth me to be spoken at home and the Dorthea me for the public, but in this case, the public also hides the private."

"Sounds a lot like the old man's sort of resistance strategies."

"Exactly."

"So, what's the *Archaic Record* have to say about drouth?"

"Drouth is a weather condition that causes intense dry spells."

"You mean, like a drought?" he asked.

"Yes, but in a really extreme form it brings about burning. Throughout the A R, light is equated with astral light, and the burning is said to be caused by waking Imogravi. The counterpart of Drouth, or *Water Siege*, is a flood so vast the entire globe is consumed in water. In its most extreme form, it's called the *Great Cataclysm* or the *Second Flow of Agonie*. 'And the world shall burn before the Last Cataclysm' is a prophesy from before the creation of Malkings even. In this time there were prophecies and, apparently, dragons. In a bean pod, first everything burns, then once its burned, it all floods. At this point, flood no longer means just water. They use the phrase *a flood of matter*. My guess, and it's irrelevant because it is just

7

a guess, but a flood of matter suggests something that can be burned, so I think the cycle is unending. All things burn, they flood, they burn again, and on and on. The passage is probably metaphorical of something, but who knows what, and it doesn't really matter. The letter is a threat, which must be predicated on two things. One, knowledge that I am familiar enough with the AR to contextualize the quote (which alone is more than enough to guarantee my being tortured into suicide); and, two, knowledge of a secret, my real name, which ostensibly was known only by me and my parents..."

"We have no way of knowing what happened—"

"Don't patronize me. Even if they were tortured, they knew so much subversive shit, they could have gone for years without betraying the secret of my name. Anyway, it just struck me maybe that's why they were arrested in the first place. It's all moot anyway, since we know that somebody else knows, and now they know we know, et cetera, et cetera. But never mind. Malkings are indifferent to taking mortal lives, and the same indifference prevents them from ever understanding mortality."

"We haven't been accused of anything, and that note was just a note, not a summons. Your folks were tough as hide and totally principled; it's unlikely they leaked your name. I hope you know how lucky you are to have had Ed and Millie for parents. Imagine growing up with the belief that conforming to Malking rule was for the best?"

"Your parents are lovely people, Gale."

"Lovely and brainwashed."

"No one is free. *Nobody.*"

"In any case, how else could BRRAS know about Drouth? Maybe they wired Ed and Millie's apartment. Not really the BRRAS way of doing things. And since your parents did blow up the portico of the Lineal Descendant's Palace, we'd know by now if BRRAS had any interest in stopping The Mortal Guard."

Dorthea gave up staring at the ball of paper and returned to her food. She said, "You know how we've talked about the portico thing being a way of protecting me? Once I'm labeled a terrorist, the Malkings have no need of me. I'm a known quantity. That'll probably come in handy."

"Telepathy was already bureaucratized."

"Barely. All we know is what Calf told us. If true, they were understaffed and undertrained."

"Even still."

"Okay, what's your point?"

"It could of been one of us in the Guard."

"You think that's any more likely?"

She looked incredulous, but he knew she'd already taken the possibility to its upsetting conclusion.

"Your dad was so close to everyone in the cell. Your mom too, but Ed, he was our leader and something even deeper. We'd gladly do anything for him, and he respected all of us despite the responsibility that put on him; well except for maybe Lug Nut."

Dorthea allowed a half smile.

"We looked up to him, and he led us through one crazy stunt after another. And him? To him we were all equals. Isn't it possible that at some point he told someone the secret of Drouth?"

"You're right. It's possible."

Moving her plate aside, she uncrumpled the mimeograph, smoothed it out on the table, and went back to bed.

9

2

Library (1)

i

AR, "before the Age of creation"

The first mystery language cast nine plates of amber gold upon which the new rain fell. Small waves followed in its wake, small authors who we say are *unexistent*: the thing, the ruffian, the spire, the seven-spoked wheel, the fourteen-decimal quotation. These authors composed einrichtung's first role. In unison they tell us the flint that was mild in order to become hard was first mild; this being possible not because it is and then is not but because it can never be.

Our unexistent authors employed specific builders for the neighborhood of lower surfaces. They called their creation the net of the impossible, and its sole purpose was to catch Imogravi. Catching Imogravi is synonymous with destroying Imogravi. The truth of this cannot be known. Were Imogravi caught, the universe would begin again, postponing the age of creation until the re-formation of the second first mystery language, the second nine plates of amber gold, and the second new rain. Did the authors know Imogravi and the truth of Imogravi? Does the absence of Imogravi prove the impossible is not yet impossible? Does the absence of Imogravi prove we already exist within the second first universe?

11

And following, are we haunted by the echo of the first? Will there be a second Imogravi and a third first mystery language? How long will the echo last?

One author asks, How much of Imogravi can we catch? Another replies, Imogravi cannot be divided: Imogravi will be captured none or all—nothing less, nothing more. Hence one grasps the origin of the phrase, exactly Imogravi.

The planets came from seizure and relinquishment, habit, and chaos. Imogravi emerged from their opposition. Imogravi accelerated the grouping and distribution of inception and decay, beginning with the first growth exhibition, which was, according to the authors, far-fetched—as far as the sand, as far as the weather, as far as every emptiness. Witnesses called the project outlandish. And once the first fruit had grown, degradation swept it away to meld with the dust and exhaustion, engraving on the face of all possible outcomes, Nothing is beyond destruction. The truth of this was recorded in a provisional language that holds the only effable secret of Imogravi and its five authors: I eat flat surfaces and Agonie. If this is known, all knowledge will pass away; if not, you shall count numbers until they crumble into stone.

Silent voices called Imogravi the kite of fire and the seven-spoked wheel.

The empty fortress named the minor gods within Imogravi the tender rocks, the tiny lives, and the sieved containers.

Small colors cannot read or write, cannot hear or speak, cannot live or die, cannot bend or remain straight.

The *Archaic Record* includes more things than are.

The *Marginalia* is a work without end.

Imogravi was the constructional strength of the cosmic spool.

Imogravi was no one's rival on the battlefield when bonded to the Seven Threads, its only true siblings. During fierce fighting, as the air became dense, threatening to crush its weaker brethren, Imogravi flew to their aid. They bent low, shielding their eyes, stepping through the torrent of molten air encircling Imogravi. They found refuge between its scales, like flaxseed in hoarfrost. Iron ringlets issued from the mouth of the thing that came before all gods. With a steady breath of fire, Imogravi welded its siblings to the rings, forming a circle of iron and flesh. From below, the nearly immeasurable expanse of battle, with its flooded empires and soot, was miniaturized in the shadow of Imogravi and the Seven Threads.

The Seven Threads represent the seven forms of magnetism generated by the cosmic spool. They are known as presence, lack, ardhanaarinateshwara, more, less, light, and loam. All things can be found in their coincidence. Practitioners of the final science call *the'real* a sensuous effect of the Seven Threads' hidden behavior, manifesting as the multiple valences and modalities of their movement. For some the real is simply the strength. But as old bodies with abnormal teachers demanded new phenomena, Imogravi created a system of the real, emphasizing the roles of management, inspection, and accountability.

ii

ROOT-RACE LEANINGS

Professor Wrengold paced between stacks, removing books at random. As random as random could be. She felt her agency leaving its mark at each step, each innocent gesture marking the dust. And yet something random *was* at play, however miniscule, however girded in unconscious calculation. The conventional methods that ruled her first three books, all written here at the Library of the *Archaic Record*, had need of disruption. She wished to take aim and drag them out of their complacency. *Inside the Grid* documented the New Rain, a cult living autonomously in the uncultivated jungle occupying a wide swath of the Sixth Circle. *The Rite of the First Sorrow* made an epistolary journey through the earliest, esoteric order within the trade guilds. Rather than insinuate herself into a group founded on secrecy, she began with a series of correspondences. They were far less guarded in that format. *In This Medium We Speak*, a series of speculations on the changing role and significance of the written letter, received more criticism than praise. In particular, they took Wrengold to task for the claim that letters were a primitive mode of psychic exchange. *Psycheëpestelia*, as she coined the phenomena, disappeared when authors became aware of the letter's *physical form*. Further, she speculated the telepathy and clairvoyance recently exhibited by high-valence Malkings would follow the same course when recognition of their physical forms occurred after a Grid-wide sensory awakening or a breakthrough in *Archaic Record* hermeneutics.

The most direct criticism came from a mortal. The freed-Rooter Dr. Frame had achieved the unthinkable: professional respect amongst his Malking peers. His review of her book appeared in *Speculation*, a forum for academics to publish *loose hypotheticals*. Despite the inclusive-sounding title, reviews tended to be less than collegial. Frame wrote: "…and half-way through the second chapter, my attention waned. However, after washing the dishes and completing my Mortal Occupant renewal forms I resumed *In This Medium We Speak*. I read to the end of Chapter Three, then took a nap. What could make a book so sleep inducing? The litter of digression, mishmash, and clap-trap creates an obstacle course without design.... But these are primarily stylistic issues and fail to address the core problem: the author's thesis. Letters, we are told, began as 'a primitive mode of psychic exchange', subsequently lost due to an across-the-board shift in perception. It was at this point they transformed into the physical, textual form of which we are now most familiar. Though never stated explicitly, one assumes the moment of transformation coincides with the transition from the Primitive to the Modern. Coming from a Malking scholar who has only their immortality to fear, the thesis is like a sinkhole in the path of reason. Is there a single Animal King who recalls this psychic form of writing? The author's claim is not at all consistent with an immortal's epistemic breadth. Indeed, the claim is mortal through and through. For mortals the past becomes darkness, and in this darkness we can only speculate. The claim could as well be made by an Animal King with Root-Race leanings. Under no other circumstance can I imagine how a Malking could form an argument about the ancient past so reliant on a total lapse of memory."

Wrengold brushed the dust off a volume titled *Marginalia*: "To Never Dream/To Dream Forever; To Live and Never Die." The volumes of the A R and the *Marginalia* were not ordered by chronology, author or subject, nor by any sort of numerical system. To this day, the Kosmocratores' indexing methodology was no closer to being understood than it had been twenty thousand years ago. And since the Kosmocratores' departure, the order of all subsequent volumes was a tangle of competing interpretations of their Creators' intent.

Dates of first-mimeo were most often uncertain, and

volume numbers were absolutely willy-nilly. In her opinion, Composition, Style, Subject (CSS, or Bison's law) remained the most robust tool for determining a print date. She remembered the CSS drills from her first graduate archive seminar. Now she taught the same class. Bison had since fallen out of favor with the University, and basic predictive algorithms had replaced CSS drills. The absence of CSS in her classroom contradicted her reliance on the methodology for her own research.

"To Never Dream/To Dream Forever; To Live and Never Die," with its cardboard cover coated in cellulose laminate and red-inked body text indicated a production date after the Age of History but before the Age of Tyranny, when mimeograph ink switched from red to blue. Compared to the Kosmocratores' oblique and complex prose, Malkings' was stylistically closer to that of the instruction manual. A glance at the body text was enough to confirm the poetic title had come from the AR.

The *Archaic Record*, "Before the Age of Creation" was bound in cured langer hide, pounded with wooden mallets until translucent and waxy. The book had been mimeographed on a spirit duplicator probably within weeks of the Kosmocratores' disappearance, a second or third transcription, then, of the Kosmocratores' final words before departing.

According to the Kosmocratores, the *Marginalia* was meant as the extension of and commentary on the AR: "The *Marginalia* is a work without end," and so it became the cold storage for every subsequent publication.

Her current project, *The Fiction Within: New Readings of the* Archaic Record, sought fissures and gaps in the ancient text, a text they had long believed to be built upon philosophical and historical truths, a text with such tremendous authority, their own lives had emerged from it. At the research level, she would cull a workable pool of anomalies; each would be analyzed and processed by the stringent *Gamut Veracity Protocol* employed by her department. According to the truth or falsehood of a sample, it would be excluded or assigned further resources.

"Before the Age of Creation" contained a compelling example of such an anomaly. The phrase *exactly Imogravi*, with the barest explanatory context, implied the reader's familiarity with the idiom, and yet, in all her years since the day of creation, Wrengold had no recollection of ever reading or hearing it spoken. She made several translations using the *Grammar of the Deities*—the antiquated primer used by the Kosmocratores' to teach Malkings language (lessons only marginally successful at first). One translation raised hopeful expectation. Retranslated as 'actual dragon beggar', *exactly Imogravi* shared several points of similarity with a folk saying still in use inside the Agro-Circles: *If beggars were dragons, all mortals would fly* (*fry* replaces *fly* depending on the region and epoch). After tracing the first use to the Age of History, well after *composition of* the *Archaic Record*, Wrengold could not prove or disprove a relationship between the two phrases. Thus it would go to her graduate students for further investigation. Disconnects between the Kosmocratores' claims of creation were common. Most infamously, in one of the later volumes of the AR, the Kosmocratores, having created the Ninth Root-Race, next created thousands of other species, beginning with the most elemental: *mold and things yet smaller;* plankton, insects, vegetables, moss, and trees. The Creation Grid was engulfed in verdure and had no shortage of mosquitoes and other bothersome insects. However, after their departure, despite the lists of many diverse examples, only two genera of red-blooded animals existed within the nine circles of the Creation Grid: the Ninth Root-Race and the langer. Langers, so called from the *Book of Names* for their lazy temperament and unclean habits, were classified into six species: the spotted langer, the red langer, water sloths, Numan's langer, the gray-haired langer, and the penny-eating langer.

Instead of continuing this phase of creation, the Kosmocratores made a last minute alteration to the Malkings' physiology, turning each into a virtual zoological slide show. Valences—ever-shifting images of red-blooded animals, overlapping, morphing into one another, appearing and disappearing over every Malking's body—took the place of the species named in the *Archaic Record*. Indeed, valences came to define and reinforce Malkings' rigid social hierarchy. In some it was stronger than others. High-Valence Malkings were presumed superior. Low-Valence Malkings were presumed to have difficulty managing authority. With the exception of union clerks and janitors, few low-valence Malkings made it inside the Admin District.

The delineation between high- and low-valence contradicted the fundamental tenet known as the Immortal Career Track, which held that each Malking—immortal and all created at the same moment—should strive by their own determination to change careers every three to five hundred spans, with the expected result that eventually all citizens would know all possible careers. The Admin Bureau for Cultural Infrastructure founded the University as a training ground to accommodate these transitions. Many citizens held to the tenet, but it was enforced by an unmonitored honor system, and even the Malkings' innate tendency to conform was no deterrent to those with greater ambitions. Eroding further the Immortal Career Track, the highest positions within the First Circle Admin District were permanent, to be held forever by high-valence Malkings. For ordinary citizens, knowledge of this created an unerasable germ of doubt whose future impact might only be known by an Assemblier's forecast.

Wrengold herself had not been a strict adherent, for which she endured periodic bouts of self-recrimination. This she blamed on an early career as a nurse during the first Rooter genocide. All told she had had a higher than average number of careers. Since becoming a professor over two millennia ago, she'd given it little thought.

Why didn't the Creators elide the bestiary from the AR or simply fulfill its promise? Scholars and laymen alike had been tackling the question for eons, generating more commentary than any other section of the ancient scripture. One of the more enduring ideas came from Councilor Cowe during the early days of exegesis: "We were taught by the Creators themselves the *Archaic Record* is a vessel of spiritual guidance. We were also taught that the *Archaic Record* is a resource for our understanding of technology and magic. This knowledge is not handed out like curtains made from pounded langer skin. To understand we must interpret. That is, the primary meaning must be turned less opaque before the secondary meaning may be ascertained; likewise the secondary meaning must be turned less opaque so the tertiary meaning can be ascertained, following the quaternary meaning, and so on. The Creators taught us that each passage houses twenty-two levels of meaning, and each level provides coded data, hidden knowledge, and insight to reward us in the varied aspects of manufacturing culture. If we are, then, to so criticize the Makers for failing to complete their task or showing a lack of foresight by departing before completing the task of creation, aren't we ignoring the purpose, the very utility of the text? And can we afford to criticize before we've reached the twenty-second level of meaning? Rather than concern ourselves with the veracity of a passage, shouldn't we first learn its depth? Let me say, in the final count, after every query has an answer, veracity is meaningless."

Since its composition fifteen thousand years ago, Cowe's essay had influenced nearly every subsequent reading. Dissenters claimed the essay's impact went far beyond the field of exegesis. They argued the clause *veracity is meaningless* gave the ruling elite a way to justify their stranglehold on knowledge and power.

After Dr. Frame's review of *In This Medium We Speak*, colleagues noticed its ill effect on Wrengold. Most assumed the reason lay in being taken to task by a mortal.

"You know it's just the administration going soft by letting those vermin into our house."

"How could that two-legged langer know anything about immortality?"

"Wrengold, hold fast to your station. Don't be swayed by such an anomaly. It's beneath you. It's beneath us all."

In fact, it was the accuracy of the review that hurt, specifically the psychological observation at the end: "The claim could as well be made by an Animal King with Root-Race leanings." Had her other books been a blind testament of her forbidden self? Her fear turned toward shame imagining each book a failure, an exercise in personal dishonesty; though in turns her shame turned to exaltation at the thought of being discovered.

Professor Wrengold was not, nor could she ever be a she, but at certain hours she revealed her desire for the impossible. Malkings had no experiential or biological concept of male and female, though some were drawn to one or the other, as if bearing an innate gender. The clinical term for the phenomenon was *gender affect disorder*. Wrengold and others modeled their affects on the gendered mortals. The practice was not illegal or even forbidden. It did, however, carry a stigma that forced the community into a self-imposed culture of secrecy, one quite different than the Rite of the First Sorrow who flaunted it. Rather, the gender affect community sought to exist without a ripple of suspicion from those on the outside. While preserving such a condition was impracticable, the majority stayed the course. Public exposure came on several fronts: gender affects publicly renouncing their association with the community; moles from the news media or the Admin District; and, most recently, a group within the community who believed the culture of anonymity should be replaced with public integration, since without direct confrontation they'd spend eternity living by night, wearing the masks of genderless Malkings during the day.

If the polls were any measure, citizens found gender affects distasteful, even obscene. Wrengold speculated that enclosing the subject in a rigid opposition between public and private granted citizens vicarious access to the forbidden. And conversely, the public shame and judgment surrounding the deviant culture helped make it possible in the first place. Thus, although she understood the rationale of going public, the possibility of total obliteration made the risk too high.

Waiting for the 7Q Cross train, Wrengold teetered between *it* and *her*, *Professor Wrengold* and *Elizabeth Luden*. A vertigo that only worsened by being in a public space. She sought refuge in the majestic architecture of the Library of the *Archaic Record*. Attached by tunnel to the western end of the University, the Library rose stories above the surrounding Admin buildings. It was built in the earliest period, before the Kosmocratores' departure, and they oversaw every stage of construction, from drawing the blueprints to casting the blocks smelted from their lead teeth. Every building inside the First Circle—except the University—was built this way, and yet the Library stood apart from the rest. Its size not only bespoke the length of the *Archaic Record* and the *Marginalia*, but lay bare the centrality of the text to everything else inside the Creation Grid.

Her gaze became a peaceful collapse into a slowly obliterating infiniteness. The Library housed too much to know, the lead permanence, the past in and out of the future, their beginning without end, the secrets to be revealed or those to be secret forever, secrets so secret they might just as well not exist. Why create such secrets? Why store them in a building? Why divulge their existence but not their key?

The train went as far as the Third Circle where she caught a trolley to the furthest arc of the Seventh Quadrant. Wrengold considered herself lucky to have an apartment a short walk to the train. Of those working inside the First Circle, Academics were given lowest housing priority. Even so, First Circle amenities were superior to those of other circles.

Halfway across the Second, the train was packed with commuters, unusual given the late hour. When the Palace Express was full, the 7Q local became the alternate of choice. *Must be a pilgrimage to the Palace*, she thought. Many new groups had formed lately. Disciples spent the night outside the Palace praying. In the morning they'd return to resume their normal routine. They might also be going to a claiming fair, though public interest had waned ever since the end of slave claiming.

Normally, pilgrims weren't from the inner circles. Agro and trade unioners were the most common demographic. The apparent change could indicate wave of career shifts. Several thousand years ago, every Malking wanted to own their own bauble factory. The Lineal Descendant intervened by creating mandatory career paths, even prohibiting career shifts away from occupations deemed necessary to Creation Grid stability. (Ever since, when controversy arose over Admin District bureaucrats' unwillingness to change career paths, they cited the LD's decree.)

These pilgrims presented another anomalous characteristic. Most wore hats. Over the last several months she had noticed the apparent fad; tonight, though, marked the first time an association with a specific group could be made. While an obvious mortal affect, the hat remained a very noncommittal gesture. These hats in particular appeared to have been bought at a gift shop. Perhaps, then, hat wearing had percolated up from the gender underground, much in the same fashion as eating food. She smiled, surrounded by the hat-wearers, on the way to her favorite gender affect discotheque.

She asked the commuter sitting beside her, "What's your destination?"

"We're going straight to the Palace."

"Pilgrimage?"

"Oh, so much more than that. We congregate to witness the final dispersal of the Lineal Descendant. And if not tonight, then tomorrow night."

The pilgrim wore a great purple sinamay with lacquered flowers and a plume of red-dyed langer hair.

Discotheque

Tess had tackled the most obvious difficulties realizing her gender affect: male/female; sexual preference; surname; clothes—even years after her first *dressing* she still felt like a novice. To some these were a central part of their gender identity. She hoped she was one. Tess kept to the sophisticated look of the female Rooters in her department. The familiarity was reassuring and provided a foundation upon which to develop her affect.

Inside the club, the last pieces of the other life fell away, leaving Tess until the end of the night. A polyphony of mortals and immortals danced and talked over the music, a few stood alone, observing or trapped in shyness. Nearly all made the most of the place, its safety and opportunity, all of them echoing with trust and shared deception.

"Tess, you look amazing!"

Sandy embraced her friend excitedly. She whispered, "You really do look great."

"I wish I could dress as wild as you."

"You could, but then you wouldn't be Tess."

"You're right, besides, Tess is hard enough."

"Elizabeth Luden, University Girl; composed, correct, and collected."

Sandy was a receptionist at a gender affect augmentation clinic. Malkings had no reproductive or digestive organs, and compared to Rooters, their limbic system was simplistic. They had mouths, vocal cords, rudimentary lungs, and a cloaca—

but no alimentary canal. A growing demand for basic mortal functions followed each surgical breakthrough. These included: 1) food eating; 2) defecation and urination; 3) sexual intercourse; 4) wider breadth of emotions; 5) higher or lower valences.

"Plus your valence is just great by itself. I'm considering surgery myself, you know, to give it a boost."

"Let's not talk about that here. You're actually pretty lucky. The valence thing is not all it's cracked up to be."

"Call me superficial, but I wanna look good day or night for the rest of eternity."

Standing on a low balcony, what club goers called *the safety station*, the girls watched the scene below in the company of the new, the ambivalent, and the shy. Tess had spent nearly every club night in that spot, only rarely venturing below. Twice under the influence. Opiates and amphetamines were a popular way of enhancing limbic simulation.

Sandy was comfortable above or below and rarely bothered with pharmaceuticals. She possessed full-fledged moods, a trait uncommon amongst Malkings. Tess worried Sandy's preoccupation with valences would lead to surgery, which was made all the more likely with her job at the clinic.

The girls were both female sex-neutral, no coupling, sexual or otherwise, with either gender or gender affect—considered by many by many to be a transitional stage. The post-transition variations were so numerous, her head swam. An affect was never simply a choice between one thing or another. Male/Male, Female/Female, Male/Female were considered foundational pairings. Though pairings between Neutral Males or Females were not unprecedented, sexual Male/Male, Female/Female, or Male/Female were more common. The implicit constraint present in all Sex/Sex-Neutral relationships was one-sidedness. The Gender Sexual's love had to be unrequited, otherwise the love object stopped being Gender Sex Neutral. Tess had seen this happen with disastrous results. The Gender Sex Neutral became a Gender Sexual when the partner's advances became attractive. But the switch was a turn-off to the primary Gender Sexual. The secondary Gender Sexual was left sorting out how capitulation could end in abandonment.

For some Gender Sex Neutrals, the arrangement worked and usually played out in two possible ways. Either the Gender Sex Neutral participated in, encouraged and, one assumed, benefited from the attention of the Gender Sexual; or the Gender Sex Neutral ignored, dismissed, and discouraged the Gender Sexual, a desirable arrangement for each party. In the extreme, these two modes were easily confused with another very different configuration: the pairing between a Gender Sex Neutral who reciprocated sexually but remained Gender Neutral and the Gender Affect Sexual whose attraction endured despite the partner's deviance. One Gender Sex Neutral/Gender Sexual couple introduced a sexual element to their relationship—like an excursion—and survived, even claiming the Gender Sex Neutral/Gender Sexual configuration remained unchanged. Another example: A Gender Sex Neutral publicly rejected the Gender Sexual partner. The Gender Sexual began stalking the Gender Sex Neutral. The community became concerned, but when asked, the Gender Sex Neutral expressed surprise and assured them nothing was wrong.

Some Animal Kings preferred Rooters and every other possible combination had been explored: Gender Sexual-Female/Male Rooter; Gender Sexual-Female/Rooter Female; Gender Sexual-Male/Rooter Male, Gender Sexual-Female/

Rooter Female, Gender Neutral/Rooter Female, Gender Neutral/Rooter Male, et cetera.

And those were the combinations of two.

Tess knew the possibilities were endless, and the unfolding was a part of what drew her in, yet she preferred to be a witness not an actor. The balcony provided this opportunity: to watch, to remain above but not wholly separate from the event.

3

belief, bureaucracy &
the creation of knowledge

i

"The scandalous Text of the False Imogravi"

ll races—mortal, immortal, unexistent—their respective deputy races and every side branchlet, these are subject to the same cleansing. Prove this with an open shadow of twilight and the triangular view that yearns for things past. Let them see it, let them collate the knowledge of cyclic atomization.

If an observer, given over to unity, sees the tangential similarities between grief and Agonie, the vision may inflict damage on the most familiar surfaces. To leave is to know everything: the absolute kingdom, the zero-point, the thing we call *bulk*.

Understanding the neutral axis of conflagration and anything rent asunder by flame shows Imogravi is within us. This is a call to stop walking.

The neutral axis is a point proven to be without a center.

The neutral axis is a term meant to describe the restriction of separate arrangements.

The neutral axis is the location of agreement between two errors (i.e., the *doctrine of allowable failure*).

These axioms will find their own transformation across nameless diminishing planes.

The First is never imagined, for the student is composed of lies, smoke, and clouds forced into the waiting sky. They believe in beings that rest atop their own homespun grouping, all tenacity surrounded by mortal weakness. A lack of unity may manifest as perplexed impulses and a vision of unexistent aspects. This becomes false knowledge—primitive, astray, stupid, and alone without hearing.

A lack of unity will be used to quantify the release and constriction of particles.

You may run towards the unexistent authors, but during the window of this transgression they become Zerkleinert, the small forgotten seeds we grind to paste.

The uneven mountains, the impact of rocks: You must acknowledge the way teachers are surrounded by fear. I sit beside the provisional language, my own myth, my own techné, the language of disease. There is no release. I can no longer fly.

The primitive is to think.

The primitive requires the regulation of death.

The primitive cannot sustain the breadth of being. In the provisional language, myth is outside the system and the state. Myth cannot be known as such. It will be revealed as event or inconsequence. Thousands of years later, after the transfer of facts, myth surrenders to the outward flow of the law, the Agonie, the unrest. To this we are indebted. For this we reach into nothing and follow its wake.

LOB

Lob held the position of senior secretary for the Bureau of Root-Race Affairs and Security. Lob's office, Surveys and Assessments, was tasked with the monthly report on Root-Race relations for the Lineal Descendant. Collated from a range of sources—including work by other bureaus—the report documented the disposition and activities of the Ninth Circle, new alliances, broken alliances, turmoil, new causes, mechanical innovation/obviation, abandoned plans, group perceptions, sustainability, citizenship, suicide, et cetera.

Two floors below, the Root 9 Preserve managed public works for the Outer Ninth: sewer, garbage, pest control; utilities; and overall maintenance of building infrastructure. By mandate, the Root 9 Preserve was a branch of Grid Utility, but over the centuries BRRAS had methodically weakened the Preserve's relationship to its parent institution. In the hands of BRRAS, Root 9 engaged in tasks more akin to intelligence than maintenance: surveillance, sabotage, work delay, subterfuge by favoritism and exclusion, misinformation, et cetera. A policy of reward and punishment, repair and neglect became the Preserve's signature. Bottom line: The compliant retained regular toilet repair and mold removal; others did not.

Composing the monthly report required weaving disparate information sources into a broad narrative, highlighting the material germane to subsequent analysis and to the presumed preference of the Lineal Descendant. Upon completion, the report was delivered to the Palace by blind courier. As new data emerged from the piles of folders that made even the short walk to the exit an obstacle course, occasional updates were required. These Lob would communicate via tele-link directly to the Lineal Descendant, then later mimeograph as a part of the monthly appendix.

Lob fiddled with a white lever protruding from a large toaster oven resting precariously on the Secretary's desktop. The pile of documents tilted the toaster off-kilter, hiding the word *Deluxe* embossed on its side. Why had the device come here and not to another office, say, Secretary Yak's, who was more at the development end of things? The smooth, white shell suggested either lacquered wood or anodized lead. The purpose of the device? To facilitate Rooter meal preparation.

In appearance, the lever resembled a light switch. In function, though, the two were quite different. The light switch controlled an inherited technology; the toaster switch a derived technology. A distinction all Malkings had been taught to recognize. A distinction embedded in a larger set of distinctions: magic versus technology, the many conditions of each, and the rule that, in turn, neither should be confused with creation. Technology was revealed in the designs bound inside the *Archaic Record*. A full third of the Administration of the Lineal Descendant, Its Fellow Citizens, and Mortal Charges was occupied with the task of decoding the *Archaic Record*, with special emphasis placed on new technologies. Magic was learned in a similar manner. The mystery of creation was neither technology nor magic and study of it was forbidden. Lob understood not why this was so.

Some magic was inherent, like communicating via tele-link or the power of telepathy. A somewhat unreliable psychokinesis had arisen from the trade guilds—*Labor saving without losing labor*, the banners declared—which made moving the Imperial Palace less arduous, though, ultimately,

32

it was powerless to prevent the disastrous outcome. More recently, the research and development phase of clairvoyance had been tied up in court by the Assembly of Forecasters and Predictive Historians, who had an enormous stake in curtailing its deployment.

Four books composed the *Archaic Record*: the "Book of Creations," the "Book of Discoveries," the "Book of Details," and the "Book of Predictions." Any inherent power could at any minute be toppled by a breakthrough in AR hermeneutics. If the "Book of Discoveries" contained an analog to the power in question, the inherent power became an inherited power. Those who believed all knowledge came from the Scriptures replaced *inherent* with *placeholder*. "What is it to know? There is no knowing. What is a discovery? All things have been revealed. The placeholder power, the placeholder discovery, the placeholder technology, and magic, these are merely the gleanings from scripture without knowing. Veracity is meaningless, to accept requires humility and faith in our Creators. Why should they burden us with the faculty of knowing?"

Lob was not of a mind either way. Once a discovery appeared, no matter from where, it grew. Of that much, Lob was sure. Data supported the claim. There were graphs.

Rooters were forbidden from reading the *Archaic Record*, and they were forbidden from developing magic or technology. The various ruling bodies tolerated minor violations, at times even encouraged them. BRRAS allowed improvements to an existing technology that countered mortal unrest. Case in point, a resourceful young Rooter named Randy Curth completely redesigned the toaster—the Rooters' sole means of cooking food nearly twenty thousand years—by expanding the cooking area and changing the direction of the heating coils from vertical to horizontal. The toaster oven, as they called it, greatly diversified the number of cookable things, and in doing so not only made a positive impact on Rooter nutritional health, but boosted morale with a pastime most seemed quite eager to explore.

Given the prohibitions against Rooters, their innovations contradicted the notion that all technology derived from the *Archaic Record*. The Lineal Descendant abated the controversy with a screed declaring the threat a minimal one, as Rooters had merely modified an existing technology. To Lob, who rallied behind most conservative agendas, the idea that Rooters must have a technology handed to them or could only improve upon a preexisting one seemed a weak and specious argument intended to diminish Rooters' contributions to the Creation Grid.

Some blamed the toaster oven for sparking the Malking interest in food, and not without good reason. Data indicated a strong analog between the advent of the toaster oven *Deluxe*, or simply the *oven* as some were now calling it, and the first evidence of a Grid-wide interest in cooking and eating. Malkings confronted a daunting list of biological deficits to simply to mimic an act so fundamental to Rooter existence. Malkings lacked a sense of taste and smell; they had no digestive system nor the organs to facilitate the process of digestion; they had a very limited limbic system and could not, in the Rooter sense, experience pleasure. And yet, after much trial and error, many became true gourmands. The phenomenon occurred after gender affects spurred surgical augmentation, a pioneering technology to emerge as much from ingenuity as scripture.

Lob was not alone in considering the behavior perverse. Regardless of what they thought desirable, Malkings had no business eating: nothing but flesh, vocal cords and a pair of rudimentary lungs past the mouth. Regarding a rectal analog, Malkings were equipped with a simple cloaca, serving nothing more than a means of cooling during the warmer seasons.

First-generation food establishments were equipped with hydraulic buckets controlled by the diner's foot. Since authenticity became a key part of the experience, Rooter patrons were always good for business. Unfortunately, they found the buckets unappealing or, in mortal parlance, *unappetizing*. They complained as well about the consistency of food prepared by cooks who lacked the required senses. Some eateries recruited Rooters to cook, but these establishments appealed mainly to blue collar Malkings and never crossed over into the more lucrative Admin District.

Two events transformed the food service industry. First, a precocious freed-Rooter, one Archie Coop, had inherited a large collection of recipes from his grandmother. He refined them over a number of years cooking in the freed-Rooter districts inside the Fifth Circle, eventually becoming a well-regarded author of recipe books and food reviews. To Coop, the work was only preparation for a long-term goal, and once he had perfected each recipe, he approached Hinde, owner of the Rooterie, one of the Creation Grid's most successful eating establishments. It is said they sat in the corner booth shrouded by shadows and possibilities, and it was there they devised their epicurean cabal. Without witnesses, the encounter had been embellished by an adoring public:

Although his arrival was unscheduled, Coop chose a time between lunch and dinner, knowing he'd catch Hinde on break, thereby showing the restaurateur his familiarity with the workings of the trade.

"I make this appeal from one entrepreneur to another," Coop said, as he opened a briefcase and removed a thick stack of rumpled mimeographs. He placed them on the table. "These recipes are the gems of my collection. Not a single one has appeared in print. Not in the newspaper, not in any of my books." The Malking arched its brow. "With these," said Coop, pushing the stack forward, "We and we alone can overcome this blasted problem of consistency."

Hinde gestured with both hands, each the size of Coop's head, giving him the floor.

"We both know that when it comes to discipline, as with so many things, Malkings are superior to Rooters." Hinde gave a weary nod. "I propose to train your cooks and teach them my recipes till they can prepare each one to total perfection. Let me add, the dishes I present here are not just masterpieces of taste but of presentation as well. With these recipes, Malking diners will have a fulfilling…that is, a pleasurable and memorable experience with such exquisite creations placed before them."

Coop paused, taking note of the silk-screened photos of patrons hanging on the walls. A fair share of Rooters were among the laughing and toasting diners, confirming Hinde's reputation as a fair-minded, Rootarian entrepreneur.

"Well, Coop, I like the substance of your proposal, though I must clarify one base assumption. When you say Malkings are disciplined, we both know you mean conformist. This plan will work because Malkings are masters of conformity. If we are to work together, I want no euphemisms, and if we're to be partners, real downright partners, we'll do so on square terms. And if you insist on being obsequious, you can forget the whole thing."

"Right. Okay, Hinde, let's give it a go."

The second significant development came when a Malking surgeon demonstrated that a fully-functioning, synthetic alimentary canal—joining the narrow air passage to the cloaca—could be implanted without disfigurement, discomfort, or complication. Later, progress in areas originally the domain of gender augmentation—sense creation, limbic enhancement, and valence enhancement/reduction—became common. There were setbacks. Most notoriously, Dr. Sturgeon's attempt to alter the rudimentary lung into a stomach. Recipients of the experimental surgery developed acute necrosis which, in extreme cases, progressed into flesh separating from the cartilage causing discomfort if not long-term deformities and handicaps. To the surprise of Malkings and Rooters alike, the misstep led to the discovery that the Malking lung was not only functional but necessary for cell growth and replacement. All in all, though, Malking augmentative surgery quickly went from a marginalized industry catering to an underground community of, in the eyes of the public, deviants, to a mainstream success story. Lob barely tolerated the trend under any light. The behavior was wrong and defiled the dignity that made Malkings the sanctified guardians of mortals and scripture.

Food consumption was enacted in broad daylight at designated venues. The public thought it less obscene than gender affects. Lob believed the phenomena epitomized the perversion and decadence seeping into the Creation Grid. Even Inner-Circle Malkings were succumbing to temptation. In Lob's own building bloc, a collator from the Bureau, in fact, lived in union with a working-class Malking from the Bauble District. Lob did not know if the behavior was illegal; there was no question, however, that it was irregular and distasteful. A Bauble District Malking living in the Second

Circle was, technically, in violation of the Separate Equality Act. The couple made no attempt to hide the relationship or their displays of intimacies, what they called *fucking*. More shocking still, according to office gossip, Malking and Rooter unions were de rigueur.

To date, no one had been charged, cited, or reprimanded for even the most flagrant acts of pseudo-Rooter activity, be it gender emulation, clothes wearing, or food eating. Who to blame? The opinions differed and too often came saddled with their own agendas. The Anti-Rooter League argued the problem originated with the corrupting influence of mortality, especially since the early days after the reform, and its attempt to unify all residents of the Creation Grid. The League had lost credibility, though, after a prolonged campaign to make spelling Rooter with a capital 'R' illegal. Many scholars who studied the effects of immortality on Malkings argued the impulse was not so much an act of decadence but of boredom. Freed-Rooter academics, like the honorable Dr. Frame, held the opinion that the ethos of the immortal should include the desire to make constructive contributions to the Creation Grid; such an ethos would counteract the potential of immortality-based boredom, replacing it with value-based action. Regarding the transvestism of modern-day Malkings, Dr. Frame was too quick if not a bit disingenuous in his condemnation of Rooter influence. Lob had observed that freed-Rooters, especially freed-Rooter intellectuals, often espoused aggressive anti-Rooter sentiment, muddling their own arguments in the process. Frustratingly, the posturing was absolutely necessary for any freed-Rooter to maintain their status outside the Ninth Circle. Lob agreed with Dr. Frame's main argument and once again found his thinking a great asset to Malkings' own understanding of themselves.

Frame wrote, "Civic duty is nothing more than the citizenry reflecting the examples set by their leaders. Decadence and depravity may be understood according to the same rule." Lob believed the Lineal Descendant should be held responsible for the actions of the citizens. Duty and leadership were rarely discussed within the Inner Circles, yet Lob felt duty-bound to broach the subject whenever the chance arose. Unfortunately, acting on the impulse had a way of killing even the most lively conversation, leaving Lob alone, a mere spectator at parties and other casual Bureau functions.

Lob's political disposition had grown from an event now many millennia past. The second day after creation, the Kosmocratores had assigned all permanent posts within the Admin District: the Lineal Descendant, the Assembly of Forecasters and Predictive Historians, and the Circle of Nine. Lob had been one of the Nine. These positions were unique as they fell outside the Immortal Career Track. The Creators intended they be held for eternity, and over the next three thousand years nothing suggested otherwise.

The fateful event began in the Palace projection room with the Circle on Nine's quarterly report to the Lineal Descendant, including updates and petitions. A proper telepathic link produced a sensation like a magnetic pull, as if the sender's thoughts were being drawn towards the receiver. That day, the *pull* was weak, and establishing a usable link took several tries. Halfway through the report, the data stream switched direction, and the LD blanketed their delivery with a conjuring of white noise and static. Silence, then a garbled mass of rumbling, and again, a very precise, very directed silence, broken by the Sovereign some hours later: *The Lineal Descendant. Testing. The Lineal Descendant. The Lineal Descendant. I. Ah-hem. I. Long live mortal affects. I the*

Lineal Descendant enjoy many affects. I the Lineal Descendant enjoys many affects. I dress. I dress with clothes. I grow flax and jute. I plant, I grow, I harvest and spin. I use my loom; I warp and woof. I produce sack cloth. I've built a tailor's shop. I draw patterns. I pin and trim. I sew with needle, thread, and thimble. And voila! A very nice skirt or pants. The reward of working with one's hands is very rewarding. I say the outcome is a miracle rivaling even the Kosmocratores' creations!

The Lineal Descendant prattled on, while the Circle of Nine, dazed, regrouped and prepared to cloak the blasphemous thought projection. They couldn't stop its issue, but they could disrupt the likelihood of interception beyond the projection room. As they readied to implement the defense, Lem, always the quietest of the bunch, enacted a reply in kind to the Lineal Descendant's oration: "Freedom to mortal affects or die!"

The remaining eight split into two groups, half to contain the LD's scandalous confession, the other to repress Lem. They attacked with a barrage of psychic babble, potent enough to leave a stadium of Rooters befuddled for weeks. They neutralized the LD's monologue with *fragmentation* and a technique they called *cocooning*, wherein the resulting fragments were wrapped in a neutral field of non-meaning language strands. A citizen passing within a few miles of the Grid might register the gist of the LD's rant, but the gist itself would remain virtually impossible to contextualize. And the attack on poor Lem, at such close range, rendered him or her (they never learned which) emptied of all but immortality.

Subsequently committed to the Asylum, Lem was diagnosed with *gender affect disorder*. Later, when the prescribed therapy failed, the diagnosis was amended to *gender affect psychosis*:

"The patient is unresponsive to all treatment known to the inheritors of the Kosmocratores' purpose and shall be housed inside the Asylum until the end of eternity."

Proper obfuscation of the Lineal Descendant's thought projection would have required the attention of the entire Circle of Nine. Lob realized that even without Lem's interruption, the effort would have failed, due to the LD's confession weakening Lem's resolve. In any case, a wounded signal limped across the Creation Grid.

For the most part, those with developed psychic abilities lived and worked inside the first three Circles. The damage, then, was contained to the upper echelons, preventing a potential Grid-wide crisis of consciousness. Lob knew full well the hazardous downside. The same audience that could parse the data had the power to turn it to political advantage.

A vague sense that the Lineal Descendant was gender affected settled inside the first two Circles. As no one held concrete knowledge of the LD's *situation*, the incomplete data integrated seamlessly into a broader set of preexisting speculations. Ultimately, shards of the confession filtered down to the general population in the form of gossip and hearsay.

Shortly following these events, Lob resigned. The exit of two from the Circle of Nine was absolutely without precedent. The positions had been assigned by the Kosmocratores, making each an inheritance from the Creators themselves But after learning of the Lineal Descendant's predilection, and knowing the Creation Grid's highest judicial body was now complicit, Lob could not carry on without an utter loss of purpose and well-being. The Circle of Nine held a series of hearings, but in the end their resistance gave way, and they approved the request. Lob's written resignation was rubber-stamped *Circle 9 Extraction Request: Approved.* After which Lob was free to join the ranks below and soon settled comfortably into the mid-level management position at the Bureau of Root-Race Affairs and Security.

4

The immortal

i

Marginalia, "new texts for learning: the lineal descendant"

The Kosmocratores selected the One as the first servant to all gods and master of all else. The One is also known as the Sovereign, the Lineal Descendant, the Prime Mover, and the Queen, depending on the intent of the invocation, the constraints of the season, and the depth of Agonie felt by the knower. No mortal or immortal may look upon the Lineal Descendant. The One must remain singular in the most absolute sense to live out eternity inside the Imperial Palace built from the Kosmocratores' lead teeth.

The ten thousand Kosmocratores speak in unison:

To build a lasting order, we hand you the House of Shadows. All truths can be demonstrated. Demonstration is a benchmark of determining that which is true and that which is false. A falsehood cannot be replicated in the world. If a falsehood is replicated it is no longer false. Study the blueprint for a house. If we build a house following the blueprint, we say the house is true. If a second identical house is built following the same blueprint, we say the blueprint is true. The blueprint and the house: Together they compose the House of Shadows.

Remember the adage, 'The seam runs deeper than the ore'. You are the guardians of the Root-Race. To think the roles reversed is called sacrilege or sedition. Change ushers back the chaos that once strangled our universe. We are the guardians of creation; you are the guardians of all else. This is the House of Shadows. A shadow within a shadow.

Since the Kosmocratores' departure, we ask the question, What does it mean to rule over shadows?

ii

I, the Lineal Descendant

I, the Lineal Descendant, the Animal King, the King of Kings, sovereign over Malkings, the Root-Race, and all mortal beings of the Creation Grid, I ready myself beneath the humble guillotine. The blade will swing sideways, and I stand within its arc. We are situated somewhere inside the lead walls of the Imperial Palace. I thread a short length of rope through the locked trigger. The neck-high arm of the pendulum—a long affair cocked tight against a coiled spring—terminates at the disk-shaped blade, by which, momentarily, I shall be decapitated. Surrounding us, my living chamber is a chaos of books, policy reports, and scribbled notes assembled in awkward piles on the floor. A granite throne, pushed hurriedly into the far corner, has carved four deep troughs across the soft floorlead. Excusing the swathe of darkly-dried blood on the seat and back, the throne is unadorned. Dry leadmold coats not only the walls but the books and papers too: the dust of a billion black spores and other detritus, all becoming a part of the very air.

Twenty thousand years have past. Blind Palace attendants serve me without seeing or being seen. Blind with their other senses horribly muted, these lowest of low-valence Malkings work by schedule and memory.

The ceilings are too high in this place, this Palace, higher than convenience, freedom, fidelity, solitude, need, greed, or even prosperity require. Which is to say, too high for me on the inside, and not so high for those on the outside. Their appetite is, apparently, insatiable. There are pilgrimages and serenades, love letters and hate mail. I serenade, love, and hate them all. It matters not. I've been told my Palace's spires inspired the blue spires, where, apparently the Rooters (as we now know them) spend their days, contained, out of harm's way.

Each of my nine spires punctuates the center of a massive rotunda. Nine rotundas form a circle, joined by short, arched hallways. The configuration leaves a rather large, open space in the middle, enclosed on each side by the convex, rotunda exteriors. This is my out of doors. Looking upwards, I know the limit of my senses. Anyone free to leave would say, "This place is so large." To me, who cannot, it is smaller than the surroundings. It constricts with stifling airlessness. It leverages my desire. Desire and other exaggerations.

The immensity and emptiness of the Palace has long since broken any thread mooring me to a purpose in the Grid. Do I tell you this because you are deserving?; because I am worthy?; because it serves the greater good? Imagine reason irrelevant. Imagine reason emerging from emptiness. Imagine I, the Lineal Descendant, am the sovereign of a stupid, stupid emptiness. Imagine now I am talking only to myself.

The Palace was built from the Kosmocratores lead teeth, which they shed before vanishing to a world yet even unborn. Melted inside great iron smelters, as per instructions, the molten teeth were cast into pillars and bricks, from which the

Malkings (as the mortals now know us) built the Palace and all of its arches, vaults, and spires. We worked our way outward, circle by circle, exhausting the lead by the Fifth Circle, switching to concrete and daubing thereafter. Actually, *they* did, *I* did not, yet I applauded, cheered them on, with my spirit guiding their journey outward past the Ninth, while I remained locked inside a box impervious to light.

I possess the only remaining complete set of Kosmocratore teeth: each tooth bigger than my own head, each a perfect paperweight or bookend.

Completing an adjustment beneath the apparatus, I step backwards to the center of the room—just inside the arc of the blade—holding gently a thin and dangerous rope. To protect against disappointment, I call my attempts experiments, experiments to determine the limit of immortality. Later, the Creators willing, it'll be called something else; or someone else will call it something else. Truly, then, our greatest hope shall be fulfilled: to forever change the Grid. Imogravi willing, et cetera.

My sole connection to the outside is by thought; great ballooning thoughts; they go out; others come in. Communication is, after all, an exchange. An exchange of ideas, of desires (oh, dreaded desire!), of directives. Twenty thousand years hunting me down, endowing me, giving me the time to learn everything forwards, then backwards. I stand inside the arc of my blade. I listen to *A Prelude to The Kosmocratores' First Creation: The Language of the Spheres*, composed of hissing and silence. I cannot say if it could be heard by ears. I cannot tell if it's on the inside or the outside. I can say with certainty it exaggerates the emptiness of this place.

Five tall stacks of dog-eared paper obscure my desktop, dominated by the mimeo *Inverting the Stationary Residue of Decay*, an analysis and discussion prepared by the Bureau of Root-Race Affairs and Security, with focus on the consequences of disruption, turmoil, and other damage to inter-relationships between fellow Rooters and their social fabric—special emphasis on solutions and new policies. The study reviews a number of power-related biomedical factors as well, including conventional and mathematical demography, mortality, sanity, and usefulness. Tertiary topics: residential distribution, more turmoil, systematized reproduction, sexual relinquishment, accelerated aging, retirement forfeiture, imposed order and belief, intergenerational jumbling, and the biodemography on other planets. A disproportionately long appendix gives the preliminary results of three geographical studies indicating a rapid expansion of sand and cold—or the decrease of water and heat—beyond the Grid.

I glance sidelong at the paper topography of my desktop, trying to determine if reading the report makes a difference to my life or the lives of others. My thoughts are diverted by an incoming transmission: someone from **BRRAS**, what I like to call the Bureau of Disgrace, Neglect, and Suppression. As a final act of my endless power, I might make the name official. I'll broach it to Lob during our transmission, for it must be Lob by the fear and irrepressible distrust in the thoughts—of me.

Secretary Lob.

Your Majesty.

How may we facilitate your service to the Lineal Descendant?

Your Majesty, we've detected activity in one of the blue spire housing blocs.

Undesirable activity?

Perhaps, my Lord.

I wouldn't expect anything less.

No, my Lord.

What sort of activity?

Belief activity, my Lord.

I see. That is unusual. What belief exactly?

We've detected a belief in dragons.

You're right, very unusual. Thank you Secretary Lob.

Your Majesty, may I add you have my continued and unfailing devotion. I remain your servant.

As it should be, Lob. But it's always good to hear.

Thank you, my lord.

To the matter at hand: I give the rope a light tug, and the blade swings free from its release. The contact is forceful and direct. The blade moves unimpeded through its willing target. Having completed its arc of trajectory, the blade hits a rubber bumper on the side of the machine's carriage and reverses direction, meeting with no resistance, where a second ago it had, returning safely behind the release mechanism's one-way latch. And I? I who am always up for anything? I am severed horizontally at the head stalk. The two pieces fall; one remains still on the floor; the other rolls adventurously across the lead flagstones.

iii

An invisible hand

The head was too familiar and too strange. Either way, it had inarguably become separate from the rest. My head. My head had become inanimate, a thing, like a stick or a cobweb. And the body? Was there a relationship between the two? The moment grew more puzzling as the identity of the *thing* became more certain, not so much that the head was recognizable, but that *I* could recognize it. By what faculty? If the senses required to see were housed in the decapitated object, how could it perceive itself? *Myself,* I thought. My head. Flat on the floor the leadstone stabbed cold against my body. And nothing yet from the abandoned globe across the floor. No sense; no thought. Mute and motionless as well. I reached outward touching the object, sensing it yet not seeing the hand! Motility and invisibility? To see one head meant the presence of another, so with some hesitation, I grasped at where the seeing eyes must be seeing and found the familiar features that were me. How in hindsight can you not be just a little piqued at recalling the Creators' warning, *The desecrated body shall disappear; aye, but it will neither vanish nor ever wash ashore.*

Not so long ago I regarded immortality a blessing. Malkings are the immortal mortals; they are bound to Earth but will never die. They will know their author once in the beginning and never again thereafter. The Malkings have no adoptive parents. No one to offer instruction and assurances in times of doubt. No cradle or loving caress. No surnames. And of course in the midst of all else, these orphans will never know an end. And whether they believed it or not (the belief was not encouraged), their very mortality meant Rooters were assured a death and a continued presence after death. These mortal mortals will survive through nameless, timeless reincarnations. Conversely, it is immortality itself that denies Malkings the same. All Root-Races have been and always will be subjugated by the Malkings, and as the eternal hours wear on, each man, woman, and child will die as many times as it takes to surpass their masters. In fact, if the millennia of rumors are any indication, only the supremely abject specimens are denied the ultimate end. I recall a rather ambitious Predictive History from the Assembly that gave a few concrete numbers regarding frequency and extent: ninety percent—by conservative estimates—will gain passage to the Unexistent Light, even if it takes a hundred thousand life cycles to do so.

I freely acknowledge my grim assessment of immortality is informed by a chronic boredom that's plagued me for over ten thousand years. The first millennia of rule was peaceful. The Malkings were happy working, living out their careers, becoming specialists in numerous fields. Many took to the notion that, eventually, they would become masters of all occupations. (To this day, the Immortal Career Track maintained a strong standing in the polls.) Then what? A career generally lasted three to five hundred spans before a Malking began again as a student or an apprentice. Exceptions existed, beginning with my own self and my eternal (some might say *infernal*) appointment as the Lineal Descendant. I will never have a career change. Those appointed to the Circle of Nine, our highest judicial branch, would, with rare exception, retain their appointments forever. Alas, one lost from a violence intended to protect the normative values of decency and the incorruptibility of the Inner Circles, the other, for far more personal reasons, from the recognition that the normative values of decency were hollow idols of the past, that the Inner Circles were not only corrupt, but corrupt to the very core (the *core*, that would be me). Within the Assembly of Forecasters and Predictive Historians, the nine Assembliers of the First Assembly were intended permanent appointments. They lost one after a rather sordid affair concerning the whereabouts of the first eight Root-Races. Why were we surprised when the master plan produced casualties? One is drawn to the notion that Malkings, generally, lack curiosity.

Rooters have created a culture of knowledge that compounds through their consecutive generations. One day we may pay dearly for endowing them with such power. Had the Makers foreseen a time when the Lineal Descendant was deposed by the Ninth Root-Race? Had the Forecasters forecast this outcome? Once, the Queen, that is I, was very nearly deposed by her subjects. A rebellion against the LD in which Rooters and Malkings unified to fight was completely unimaginable. The most obvious feature of the relationship between the two is their differences; differences so profound, so much a part of their respective weaves, they are bound by opposition and misunderstanding. The recent implementation of segregated welfare districts only codified an existing separation. Though occasional agreement did occur. The welfare blocs were built on the remains of a much more diverse historic architecture. And no one liked the blue projections. Eighth Circle property values slumped almost immediately. Rooters and Malkings alike complained of something they called the *blue chills*.

More Rooters lived in the Ninth Circle now than before welfare was institutionalized, which can be accounted for by an increase of mortal births; a subsidy program that, however flawed, provided for basic mortal needs; the end of slave claiming; and an overall drop in the number of Rooters exiling themselves outside the Creation Grid to the Surroundings. A small but apparently increasing number of final incarnations and suicides were becoming statistically relevant and would likely impact the next census. How suicide played out with regards to reincarnation was unknown.

I was sorting out the ontological relationship between the *me* and the *not me* when several langers come into view. They converge on my severed head. My severed head! With nonstop chattering and a clawed-tumble over control of the rare carrion, they set about eating the spongy meat off the large, roundish cartilage. It truly was an empty, empty life.

After the first ten thousand years of my tenure as the LD, I had endured an isolation greater than the compound isolation of a thousand generations of Rooters. At this point, the Palace became bigger and emptier-seeming. (It truly was enormous and could house a legion of Kosmocratores, yet beyond the staff of blind servants, who themselves were expert at not being seen, I had no company at all.)

My sense of well-being took a nosedive; and so began a five thousand year arc of self-pity, catatonic withdrawal, rage, suicidal ideation, and remorse, all culminating in a series of preliminary suicidal actions. The early days of despair were a dark period not only for the LD but for the entire Creation Grid, Malkings and Rooters alike. My malaise left me so bereft of sympathy that anything outside the sleeping chamber became dark and threatening. The affairs of state lost their meaning. My sovereignty might as well have been a steaming langer turd stuck to the back of my head, assuming I had one— a head. Quite understandably my administration expressed concerned, and eventually the first-tier bureaucrats—the Circle of Nine, the First Assembly, sundry sycophants, and the goons from the trade-guilds—took control of the day-to-day policy making, becoming a de facto civil authority. I did not relinquish total control—there was no coup. Rather, they stepped into a large body of unattended responsibilities.

My depression found its nadir with a telepathic communique from the Admin District. The Circle of Nine—very courteously—announced its intention to move the Palace and its contents from the First Circle to the Surroundings, beyond the city wall.

Delays were long standing, as the trade guilds were not particularly keen on moving the Palace half a diameter across the Grid, and yet the engineering know-how necessarily made them the only candidates for the job. One assumes the Admin bureaucrats capitulated on a number of points. Meanwhile, as the start-and-stop journey progressed, I refused even a peak outside, spending most days in my unfurnished bedchamber, ensconced inside the Imperial viewing sock, a great swathe of black cloth provided so the cleaners could clean while their lord remained hidden from sight, asleep or pretending to be so. Not even halfway across the fifth circle, the entourage transporting my edifice hit a bog so vicious the entire west corner of the Palace sunk into mud from the bottom of the basement all the way up to the lead foundation plate. And so they abandoned me and my Palace askew in the middle of nowhere. Worse than nowhere. This particular inhospitable stretch of nowhere was smack in the middle of the largest langer reserve on the Grid, stretching half-way across the Fifth Circle. Quickly my over-sized, cata-wonky chateau became the number one destination spot for these lazy and malcontent creatures. The langer spends the day—and night for that matter—hanging upside down from any protrusion that will accommodate its bristled, knobby tail. While langers are loath to move, they'll gladly fling their feces at anything that does. And if by chance their paws are busy, say, peeling the backs off shit-eating gleaning beetles, the langer's marble-sized turds are projected over its dangling hind side, to roll down the curve of its back, then launch off the creature's concave head. Most hit their intended target as I pace in a melancholic trance between crowded arches, brushing off the soft, round missiles.

Five thousand years passed in this way. And upon the fifteen thousandth year of my ascendancy, I resolved to regain my rule. In the *Secret History* this period is referred to as the Age of Tyranny. Yes, the LD became a tyrant for nearly five millennia! Rooters were stripped of all substantive means of redress and legal recourse; their civil rights were dissolved; many were arbitrarily executed. It was at this time the welfare districts were created to humiliate them yet further. I banished most of the ruling echelon of Malkings and demoted the rest to servile administrative positions.

And yet not even wanton carnage and repression lifted my boredom.

Correcting the mess I'd created did prove to be something of a challenge and thankfully offered a worthy distraction. Publicly, this period is known as the Age of Reform. Privately it began my quest for the perfect suicide. Publicly I brought the ruling echelon out of exile and gave the Rooters more wiggle room. Privately I began combing the *Archaic Record* for ways around my immortality. I so longed for release, no truer impulse has been known by another living soul. The *Archaic Record* is very long. No one could say they had read the whole thing. Maybe the first three books, but not the "Book of Predictions," as new pages popped up every day. Maybe it was a trifle to them, but from anyone else's eyes the Kosmocratores' task was a monumental one. Never mind that the first three books filled twenty floors of the Library of the *Archaic Record*, never mind that from these three books civilization was drawn, never mind that every colossal truth and miraculous fact was bound within them. Never mind.

Let's look more closely at the fourth book. As no one but myself, the Circle of Nine, and Assembly of Forecasters and Predictive Historians have full access to it. (My use of *look* is therefore meant in the most lose and rhetorical sense.) But I say just look at it. Here is a text first begun sometime before the creation of Animal Kings, which provides a predictive chronology of all events to occur inside the Creation Grid, from beginning to, one assumes, the end of eternity. Where the Assembly of Forecasters and Predictive Historians work in a like-minded vein (a nice example of Rooter anatomy becoming a Malking metaphor), they, the Assembly, work in economical, very immediate chunks of time. They also manage the details, the minutia, the daily ins and outs, where the Creators' concern is the big picture, the broad strokes, the overall arc of things. And perhaps the most wondrous of all, the book is continuously updated, pushing further and further into the history of the future. Practically every day, I find mimeographs strewn about the floor like so much wheat straw. (This is a bit disingenuous as I know wheat straw only as a phrase.)

We, the three highest orders of bureaucracy, have the additional privilege of knowing this text. For me, it is damn handy for forming effective policy, if I'm in the mood. The Assembly, who are most reliant on it, have a starting point for their own work. For the Circle of Nine, the book makes evidence and opinion tertiary considerations when composing a ruling, a ruling all the more likely to conform to its predicted outcome.

Obviously a single incongruity between prediction and outcome can easily throw the whole apparatus off the course. As you might suspect, the "Book of Predictions" is often flat-out wrong, and over the millennia, the degree of error has compounded to the point where updates are often corrections or formulas to recalibrate subsequent predictions. And yet. And yet the book guides us to whom the task of rule has been bestowed.

Not insignificantly, the text's wrongness appears in unexpected arenas. Early on, I would have wagered that my behavior, given as I am to such tumultuous moods, would have been the greatest challenge to our Creators' guesswork. I soon found that I, the LD, was, in fact, the most predictable component. Indeed, no one with access to the text had anymore than the slightest impact on the text's correctness, something along the lines of a pinprick or mosquito-bite's worth. (It remains inscrutable to me how my attempts to rebel only lead history closer to its predicted conclusion. Facing an unbeatable opponent, where every loss is a humiliation, I now follow a *no read rule* and forbid myself from reading the "Book of Predictions," no matter what the occasion. Needless to say, the rule was in place long before it was obeyed—one always wants just a peak at the outcome. The concerted turn to suicide as a final solution inspired a greater discipline and resolve in my character, and even if every attempt fails, as the book no doubt foretells, I will be a better LD for it.)

An instance in which the Creators' predictive powers may prove off the mark began when BRRAS initiated a program in which Rooters were dispersed chits to buy baubles, despite the Creators' mandate prohibiting Rooters from working and possessing money. Since the beginning, baubles were sold in the first eight Circles. BRRAS offered large subsidies to a handful of manufacturers, effectively paying for the bauble doles in the Ninth Circle. The unsubsidized manufacturers—no doubt in cahoots with various factions of the Trade Guilds—formed a coalition, demanding equal consideration. Not prepared to subsidize every bauble maker on the grid, BRRAS opened up the Ninth Circle to a sort of free-market style commerce, wherein each rooter was allotted bauble tokens in the place of money, with which to purchase baubles. The manufacturers were, thereby, thrust into a fully energized and competitive market. With the introduction of lead tokens, accompanied by the requisite *chit to currency* exchange, BRRAS fully reimbursed manufacturers. This policy shift brought the Rooters one step closer to handling money, a liberty that could only be sustained by the Rooters' employment in labor. Only the unfolding of real events can demonstrate the outcome of such a radical policy.

In any case, I began looking for loopholes but quickly found that my memory and patience had gone soft. And so I dusted off the *box test*, the earliest learning tool provided by the Creators, designed to teach the newly created Malkings the basic skills required of Guardians. It contained five hundred thousand very thin lead pieces to be assembled in a thousand different configurations. The interlocking shapes created both two- and three-dimensional forms. Two possibilities of which I was particularly fond were the single-surfaced image that exactly replicated the floor upon which it was assembled and the hollow cube with an abstract relief image of the Creation Grid on each face, inside and out.

In addition, I versed myself in the tools of murder and how they might be turned upon myself. I studied the methods by which Rooters took their own lives. I made a clinical study of my own pain thresholds and the means by which to exceed them.

The grim and long-term impact of the Age of Tyranny was laid bare in *The Stationary Residue of Decay*, and the newly completed domestic policy outlined in *The Root-Race and the New Authority Hierarchy: Implementing the Age of Reform.* If I discovered my last exit, I would leave with some surety that the state might carry on safely without me.

Initially, I executed a series of exploratory attempts to determine the most promising methods. Decapitation came after numerous failures—gas, asphyxiation, poisoning, trauma by blunt instrument, and trauma by projectile. These produced enormous discomfort and disfigurement but, obviously, not death. Since none of my earliest attempts resulted in the complete separation of the body from itself, decapitation had come to stand out as the last hope. Alas.

As I've already relayed, this exercise achieved nothing more than to turn me invisible. Reviewing the list, now little more than a page of uncrossed-out possibilities, a single option stood out from the rest: disintegration. I cringed at the complexity and discomfort it would produce but readied myself for the job. Skimming the AR I happened upon the sentence, "Water will extinguish the Immortal Fire." It gave me pause. Extinguish the Immortal Fire. Indeed. If I were to reduce myself to a liquid mass, an invisible slurry—a la moi—could I then slowly reduce myself, evaporating the water (and my spirit with it), until a mere pile of desiccated flakes remained? I might build an automated device that could render the flakes and then immolate them at the highest possible temperature—maybe the old smelters stored in the basement would once again see the light of day.

iv

leadflesh

I shimmied up the column towards the langer squatting on the corbel above my desk. Its long, gray hair and watery eyes had come to inspire a longing to harm. Since our last encounter the cursed creature had been inside the cloakroom—why did the Creators' design include a cloakroom replete with umbrella stands? An old blueprint perhaps, something from an earlier universe?—hanging from a coat knob, apparently sulking. As it was not my first run-in with this particular specimen I thought it just as possible the nitwit was plotting some type of revenge, as I had earlier chucked it against my throne. This morning, for whatever reason, it reemerged, venturing back to its perch, where it had been wiling away the day defecating onto my head. (How could a diet of beetles and grass produce such copious amounts of excrement?) I had come to view him as the primary candidate for extermination. I planned to strangle it, then toss him to his fellow vermin, who, I guarantee you, would cannibalize the corpse without hesitation. Even murder was an ordinary occurrence amongst these stupid animals. After all, we're discussing the same grotesques who had eaten my head!

My murderous resolve fell lax when I realized a heightened sense must be required to hit an invisible target. Or was I not invisible to the langer? There would be vague irony if I were invisible to all but the langer. The thought brought me within a breath of forgiving it altogether.

The citizenry revered the langer—from a distance. The hypocrites had no idea. I lived with them day in and day out.

59

Why else did they put the reserve in the middle of the most uninhabitable stretch of the Fifth Circle? Was a single langer, caged or even stuffed, anywhere inside the First Circle? Were they popular pets amongst any but the most perverse? And on this point the Rooters and I agreed. In general, those of the Ninth shared a dislike of the creatures. They didn't eat them but gladly turned them into leather goods. This is particularly commendable as the Rooter diet is composed almost entirely of the mung bean. Bravo! May the handbag and leisure chair forever remain on the black market! Go my mortal artisans! Harvest the sacred langer. You have my blessing!

That said, I've heard tell of a pro-langer movement amongst the mortals. They huddle together—someplace dank and ill-lit I suspect—to conspire, moved by the fact that langers are the only other red-blooded mortals on the Creation Grid and should, therefore, be honored and protected. (Perhaps I've been led by the nose as I cannot verify a damn thing from here. I hope this is so as it's beyond me how anyone could know any love for the langer. If it is true, I proffer the following supposition, Why not love all mortal creatures? Why tolerate BRRAS's annual genocide of mosquitoes? I say, aren't they as worthy as the langer? If not guided by logic, the answer musty be along the lines of *You'd have to be a mortal to understand.* Indeed.

The little bastard remained out of reach, leering and shitting with admirable precision. (Now I became convinced I was invisible only to my self.) Casting about in this manner, a second related thought came to mind: If my invisibility extended to my fellow Malkings, I might leave the Palace and partake of the world. Suppose my valences had gone the way of my body? Detection of me would be difficult but not impossible. I would stick to the outer circles where the

Malkings' powers were more physical than psychic. (These citizens might be struck in the head with a brick and not know something was upon them.) But how could I know?

Further, I asked my self, *Why bother?* I thought without embarrassment or shame, *The answer eludes me.*

The first book of the *Archaic Record* is missing its final volume. This fact is known only by me. The unexistent volume of the "Book of Creations" is excluded from all editions except mine. I had no knowledge of it until the Creator entitled Primary Liaison to the LD bestowed upon me this mysterious tome. Indeed, the bestower was the same who spared its teeth from the great smelter, offering them to me instead as an apparent gift of farewell.

Beyond their specific functions, the Kosmocratores were nameless. We were supposed to know them as indistinguishable parts of one. Off the record, though, they were fond of adopting casual-sounding monikers coined by themselves in the hopes, I presumed, of bridging the distance between the creator and the created. As such, a bridging was impossible; the Kosmocratores were always naive in their attempts to assimilate, and their naming penchants never short of pathos. The names could be used sparingly when circumstance allowed, the terms of engagement were informal, and the outside noise the loudest. In my own experience, the Primary Liaison modestly requested that during our private meetings, I address it Generous Giver.

"I enjoy pretending," said Generous Giver, a gentle shiver moving slowly over its gray skin.

"But you truly are a generous giver my Grace. You've given us existence; you've given me your teeth, and today you've brought me the unexistent volume of the 'Book of Creations'. Indeed, generous is much too slight a term."

The shiver became an outright ripple from praise.

The Kosmocratores' departure was a sad day for us all. Their teeth had been smelted, the Palace built; we'd completed the last of our courses in Creation Grid Management, and with that they were gone, ascending skyward like so many lead obelisks thrust into the heavens. How could we thank them? How could we turn to them in times of need? All we had were the extremely long and complex set of instructions they'd left behind.

Rooters will say the Kosmocratores—like the Malkings— are genderless. Malkings will say they and the Creators are complete, and gender is merely a biological device to compensate for mortality. That is, Rooters are incomplete and would vanish without gender distinctions and a means to breed. "Primary creation beings are immortal and have no need for a gender mechanism. To say they *lack* gender is inaccurate, as mortality is a derivation of immortality. More accurately: Second generation creation beings lack immortality." So says *The Teacher's Handbook*.

The Kosmocratores had neither eyes nor ears, and their mouths served simply as a place to store their teeth. The intrinsic function of the teeth, if one existed, was never revealed. Once they fell out and the teeth were melted down, their mouths disappeared, leaving a great flat wall of gray, hairless leadflesh. Henceforth they spoke from a place beyond their bodies—*ventriloquism of the gods*, as we were fond of saying.

Big or small, admittedly or not admittedly, sanctioned or not sanctioned, willingly or not willingly, all Malkings adopt mortal affects. As created, we have few inherent personality qualities. Most were learned during the early learning period. Some call the second half of the Age of Creation the Age of Instruction. Of course, I had private tutors and was, indeed, more sheltered, less familiar with the potential embarrassments of being taught how to exist along side my peers. For those who were not me, then, much was gleaned from the early days in the classroom. The rest, what might be called the *social* or *day-to-day* components of existence, were borrowed from the Rooters: basic know-how regarding what to do and when to do it; how to read interpersonal dynamics; how to feel; how to affect desire and need; how to give; when to express anger or joy; when to mirror; when to accept loss, et cetera. In short how to emulate a range of responses not innately present in the Malking psyche. My fellow Malkings, though, are crafty in their modes of emulation and developed stratagems to avoid detection by mortals.

The charge to maintain basic mortal upkeep makes such emulation necessary. An unconscious lapse in the mortals' belief that we share a set of assumptions about existence would erode Malking authority. The Rooter psyche is complex. They organize themselves and their world by division: the self/the self's being; mind/body; empirical/theoretical knowledge/ignorance; adherence to good/adherence to bad; and so on. The self and being are intertwined but never fully integrated.

When an Animal King adopts a mortal affect for leadership purposes, it will exploit the mortal gap between self and being by utilizing the traits least desirable to Rooters, those they rarely acknowledge in themselves—anger, contempt, disgust, guilt, fear, spite, neglectfulness, selfishness, vanity, and greed for instance. Following, then, the logic concludes: If the trait is not recognized by the party of the first part, the trait's origin will not be recognized by the party of the first part when emulated by the party of the second part.

The First Circle was tasked with keeping these traits alive in Rooters, the later having no idea the strictures placed on them served a purpose unrelated to security or direct state control. Malking success rested on mortals repressing their normal negative responses to avoid being like their masters and rulers. Mortals must believe the negative response patterns associated with being oppressed originate with Malkings, which, in turn, provide the perfect foil for immortals to strategically adopt mortal affects without detection.

Unfortunately, Rooters never respond with the requisite degree of precision or predictability for Malkings to calculate exactly which traits to emulate. Further, it turns out, Malkings have their own (albeit narrow) range of emotional traits, which can become confused with that of mortals', creating what's known as *affect feedback* or *schizoid immortality disorder*.

Try as we might, we can't blame the Root-Race for everything. We've made them who they are. Now we must make ourselves into them. Gender affects are a strange exception. They borrow too much of the subject by foregrounding the central biological distinction between us and them: the need and means to reproduce. Of late, my own tendencies lean towards a male gender, though I enjoy anything that provides some alternative to the norm. In the beginning I read studies on male and female personas. I reached deeply into myself; I sought strength, intuition, and protective loyalty. I sought, as they say, my feminine and masculine sides. These were futile exercises. Gender affects are necessarily superficial. Some days I pad around the Palace in a silk nightgown, my face red-smudged with rouge, the lipstick hanging gently between two fingers. Other days I ask myself, *What if I take away the dress and the makeup? What am I then? How can an identity be forged from a few prefabricated accoutrements?* There are no answers to these questions.

The strictures on bearing witness to me, the Lineal Descendant, extends to descriptions both visual and verbal. Why did the Makers believe I was necessary? If I were tomorrow to disappear, who would notice? Who *could* notice? The invisibility of my form may be recent, but the rest of me has been this way for millennia.

The upper echelons communicate using telepathic pathways engineered by the Kosmocratores, and for all official communication telepathy is mandatory. Telepathy has two main advantages over other modes of communication.

1) Rooters cannot intercept telepathic communication, promising the free, secure exchange of classified and other public-sensitive material. Admin Malkings sympathetic to Rooter civil rights, those who freely betray confidentiality by leaking intelligence, are such a minority the risk is minimal. Besides, who cares? The likelihood of a breach is diminished further by identifying those citizens with such tendencies and blocking them from posts where sensitive information is generated, analyzed, or implemented. A large degree of overlap exists between gender affect bureaucrats and pro-Rooter subversives, facilitating the identification and control of these undesirable elements.

Implementing authority of any kind is, in my opinion, a formality. Often the best course is to simply confirm the preconceptions, even the negative ones. As I shall illustrate momentarily, not everyone in the Inner Circles agrees with this assessment.

2) Telepathy makes possible virtual meetings with the Circle of Nine, aka, *Inner Council of the Outer Domain*, who

are, ostensibly, the public face of the Lineal Descendant. Similarly, the LD can maintain direct communication between the Admin Bureaus and the Assembly of Forecasters and Predictive Historians.

It was during such a meeting with the ICOD shortly after implementing the Age of Reform when I botched everything. Petitions by industrial management organizations seeking the high court to nullify the Kosmocratores' prohibitions against Rooters joining the labor force began our session. The *Archaic Record* states, "The Ninth Root-Race shall not engage in trade or an exchange of labor for pay, but instead be forever handheld by the hands of their Lords." The industrialists asserted the text might just as well be a sanction for slave labor. It was not a new argument and often arose at the slightest rumblings from trade guilds. The winning counterpoint rested on a passage from the AR but required my signature to be binding. Later in the same chapter, the Creators return to Rooters and trade, "Some form of material exchange is not only inevitable but desirable provided the goal is to stave off turmoil. As stated earlier, maintaining order amongst the mortals is not mandatory but has the clear advantage of being less laborious—i.e., using fewer resources—than the alternative. Open commerce leads to an equality between stations or the desire thereof. (Oppressed *and* oppressor may experience this desire, the former as part of a larger desire for freedom; the later as a response of sympathy toward the oppressed.) Thus it must be underscored: There shall be no commerce between mortals and immortals. The needs of every mortal remain the charge of their masters, barring one exception. A black-market economy within the Ninth Circle will be illegal and officially condemned, but this law will never be enforced."

In the middle of Councilor Karp's recitation of the petition, I interrupted the transmission with an, admittedly, unwarranted and incongruous outburst. I had became so bored, what issued from my thoughts was an ad hoc play of associations without even a tenuous connection to Karp's surprisingly fair minded summary of the same old, same old. Somewhere in my interruption, I exclaimed, "Long live mortal affects!," which sort of caught their attention. I believed the tone of the transmission to be at once heroic *and* celebratory. I was speaking *of* the people, drawn across the surface of the grid. Hello world! Hello Grid! Finally we meet! Can a king be of the people? As much, I suppose, as an immortal can be of the mortals.

The initial response from those on the other side did little to confirm the profundity of my experience. For a pregnant moment all communications ceased. The network positively radiated an awkward silence! I sat cross-legged on the floor tossing dried langer turds into an empty gallon jug of the best mortal-made mung bean whiskey. As my reverie took its course, the silence was abruptly broken by a bodiless ally, a short transmission from one of the nine Councilors: "Freedom to mortal affects or die!" The phrase *or die* was baffling, until I blushingly recalled my own use of *long live*. The connection broke off again, only this time painfully so, something akin to bathing with a toaster oven *Deluxe* plugged in to the nearest receptacle, sans the smoke streaming from my ear flaps. Thought fragments, like shattered ice piercing skin penetrated then retracted. The mass of synaptic activity formed an inscrutable word collage. The Councilors then produced a white noise shield by whistling into cupped hands. Next came the psychic distracter in which long, thought-consuming passages of the *Archaic Record* were broadcast outward to overwhelm the telepathic airwaves. This would have required at least four Councilors, which left four, not counting my unfortunate ally, who focused on damage control and exacting some horrible punishment upon the deviant. The temerity of their action spoke to the discomfort Root-Race gender retrogressions caused high echelon Malkings. On the other side of the shields I made out 'out', 'langer', 'agony', 'rope', 'notebook', 'sequential', 'darkness', 'downright', 'toothless', 'root riots', 'turmoil', 'foundation', 'pitiful sot', 'burden', 'vacancy'.

The slim volume of the AR given me, the one upon which only I and the Creators had laid eyes (the Kosmocratores figuratively so), a volume so obscure it was not even spoken of, not with any authority anyway, was a tiny germ from which rumor and suspicion grew. For eons many assumed special books had been created for the eyes of the LD and for its eyes alone, but alas no trace of these had ever surfaced, excepting the elaborate and sometimes not so elaborate frauds that appeared every century or so. The task of the Bureau of Fraud and Speculation was to preserve a level of accuracy in public discourse, including fraudulent texts, according to an algorithm developed for analyzing thresholds of social credulity, truth, and deception. Other bureaus managed their own applications of the algorithm, but BOFAS used it to gauge the point at which false information compromised the cohesion of the social fabric. By modulating two independent variables—the State and the Public, for instance—the Bureau could quantify the amount of false information in current usage. When constant threshold parameters were applied to this data, the Bureau analysts calculated risk levels, say when false information shifted from neutral or useful to negative or dangerous. Outside factors that exaggerated or diminished threshold points were included as well. For this, the Bureau depended on other Bureaus and were well known for their impeccable relationships with other administrators. Most bureaus were relatively autonomous and cultivated long-standing and contentious rivalries. It was in such a context that BOFAS officials were either admired or disparaged as *bureau sycophants.*

BOFAS assessments and recommendations were made according to a static set of assumptions. 1) Misinformation can be divided into two horizontal categories: State Misinformation and Public Misinformation. 2) Misinformation can be divided into two vertical categories: Intentional Misinformation and Unintentional Misinformation. 3) Most misinformation created by the State is Intentional. 4) In general, Intentional State Misinformation is desirable. 5) In general, Unintentional State Misinformation is undesirable. 6) Most Public Misinformation is Unintentional. 7) In general, Unintentional Public Misinformation is desirable or not desirable. 8) In general, Intentional Public Misinformation is undesirable. 9) In most cases, excessive Intentional State Misinformation will lead to public skepticism and by turn to negative idealism and anarchic public turmoil. 10) In most cases, excessive Intentional Public Misinformation will lead to emboldened resistance and by turn to positive idealism and galvanized public turmoil. 11) In most but not all cases, Unintentional Misinformation, State or Public, is corrected with minimal resources when identified at a stage late enough to be detected but early enough to prevent a shift in public opinion.

Within BOFAS there was an unexamined suspicion that the eleven assumptions, what the BOFAS called, rather grandly, The Law, were not absolute and had innate thresholds just like the subjects of their studies. Any one of the assumptions pushed into an extreme position may no longer fit the original assumption. Slipping into another assumption would be manageable, but what if the new assumption fell outside the existing eleven? There would be no recourse. Speculation along these lines led the more curious BOFAS bureaucrats to find weaknesses in each assumption. 1) [Misinformation can be divided into two horizontal categories: State Misinformation and Public Misinformation.] Consider the possibility of a third category. 2) [Misinformation can be divided into two vertical categories: Intentional Misinformation and Unintentional Misinformation.] *Ibid.* 3) [Most misinformation created by the State is Intentional.] Unintended State Misinformation can go undetected, what is called *white* or *invisible misinformation.* 4) [In general, Intentional State Misinformation is desirable.] A maverick bureau could purposively produce harmful misinformation. 5) [In general, Unintentional State Misinformation is undesirable.] An algorithm might be written to identify the desirable effects of Unintentional State Misinformation. Something of which the Assembliers are easily capable. 6) [Most Public Misinformation is Unintentional.] What if it isn't? 7) [In general, Unintentional Public Misinformation is desirable or not desirable.] The effect of a third factor, something neither desirable nor undesirable, would be devastating. 8) [In general, Intentional Public Misinformation is undesirable.] See #5. 9) [In most cases, excessive Intentional State Misinformation leads to public skepticism and by turn to negative idealism and anarchic public turmoil.] A recent tract published by a fringe element inside the Admin District claims Intentional State Misinformation is the only way of maintaining order and productivity. Such a claim is only noteworthy because the tract was well received as it made its way throughout the Admin District. 10) [In most cases, excessive Intentional Public Misinformation will lead to emboldened resistance and by turn to positive idealism and galvanized public turmoil.] Suppose the information is not misinformation. How could the Bureau counter public turmoil over accurate information? 11) [In most but not all cases, Unintentional Misinformation, State or Public, is corrected with minimal resources when identified at a stage late enough to be detected but early enough to prevent a shift in public opinion.] Unfortunately the means of correction is typically more misinformation, which itself produces a need to be corrected.

Despite these worries the BOFAS system was highly effective, so much so, they felt their success should be followed up by a promotional campaign announcing their success to the entire Creation Grid. To champion the merits of the system and introduce a new spin to an existing poster campaign, they produced a color image of a well-groomed lawn underscored with the text Predict, Prevent, Perfect, which debuted on trolleys across the Grid, commemorating the one thousandth year of The Law. The experience led to a greater confidence amongst BOFAS officials and they made the unprecedented move of applying their methodology to freed-Rooters and the welfare Rooters inside the Ninth Circle. The results were unreliable to the point of being useless. A rift emerged amongst BOFAS analysts about whether or not their own promotional campaign wasn't itself an instance of Unintended State Misinformation deserving censorship.

In all their many centuries of service, only one fraudulent text caused the BOFAS any trouble. In the early days of the boredom that blossomed into the Age of Tyranny, I amassed remnants of the paper used for the first edition of the *Archaic Record*. I fetched the Kosmocratores' Spirit Duplicator from the Palace basement. Cleaning the machine (machines have more kinship with mortals than immortals, when it comes to repairs and lifespan) required dismantling it completely, part by part. I lubricated the moving parts and cleaned the screws, bolts and other fasteners with a sympathy for the purpose of the machine, of its earlier accomplishments and its abilities that separated it from all other machines, all other mimeo machines. I forged my text upon the now rejuvenated ancient machine and with the pigmented wax spirit master, produced a single ditto copy. This I hand-bound in langer vellum salvaged from a copy of the first Creation Grid Census, published shortly after the Kosmocratores' departure and not likely to be missed, by me at any rate. The end result was so impressive, I wished to keep the book for myself and abandoned the plan to release it into the world. Once I'd risen above this bit of vanity, the challenge became how to get it out of the Palace. Eventually I was forced to accept the impossibility of the task and resolved once again to keep the book for myself.

5

seeds

i

Marginalia, "new texts for learning: guardian"

*T*he Animal Kings are called the Guardians of Fate, for they are charged with the welfare of the Ninth Root-Race. Debate over the term *Guardian* will continue for eternity. As the emphasis will fluctuate, the meaning will remain true. A debate of degrees, the term is known to be a tripartite asmod composed of Protector, Warden, and God. The debate lies in how one understands the relationship between these aspects, more or less Protector, Warden, or God? Would the proportions be the same in all situations? For all Guardians?

No one doubts the play of three aspects; they argue over relative dominance.

The Animal Kings' perception of superiority may be grounded in a relationship to the Creators, who nursed them on distinction between immortal and mortal. Later, two points of contrast will emerge that will formalize the belief, one biological (immortal/mortal); the other political (citizen/non-citizen). The sense of superiority engenders a belief that the Guardian—whether Protector, Warden, or God—must offer provision for the guarded. Early on, policy will seek a way to guarantee the Root-Race's need for provision, which produces an even greater inequality and further exploitation of the mortal subjects. The prohibition against employment is a vestige from this era. As foment brews, the Lineal Descendant will instigated reforms, building the modern welfare state, wherein the Root-Race is prohibited from exchanging their labor for money but can do so for goods and other services. Rooters will call it the *System of Barter Welfare.* Amongst scholars, mortal and immortal, the policy will be known as the *Irony of the Guard.*

ii

Library (2)

Sitting at a Library culling bower, Dr. Frame watched the cloud through a screened window. He hesitated calling the cloud an *unusual* cloud, yet it was so nearly perfectly spherical and absolutely white, enacting a leisurely migration across the otherwise cloudless blue horizon, *unusual* was the best he could do. Being at the Library this early would likely not be a productive use of time, but his sleep had been fitful, besotted by dreams of two unnamed Animal Kings joyfully tossing him back and forth in their version of *catch.* He'd woken in darkness, then prepared and ate his cereal without turning on the lights.

University faculty and students were segregated between mortals and immortals. But since Dr. Frame's books on Creation Grid culture and economics had become so popular amongst Malking students, the dean suggested Dr. Frame design the first-ever class for Malkings taught by a Rooter professor.

74

In his published work, Dr. Frame argued that without significant growth in the consumer sector and the GNP, the Rooter welfare state would collapse. Analysts had failed to take into account the impact of reforms on the mortal population. Greater stability and a lower mortality rate meant more babies, plain and simple. And population growth meant an increased demand on the economy that set the stage for turmoil amongst Rooters if and when funding constraints resulted in cutting amenities. Such an obvious oversight epitomized Malking naïveté with regards to mortal reproduction.

To solve the imminent crises, the Lineal Descendent should, Dr. Frame argued, either reinstate *slave-claiming* or create more opportunities for Rooters to integrate into *free society*. The second option would decrease the welfare population, increase the labor force, and expand the consumer base. A third option, to abolish the welfare districts entirely and give Rooters citizenship at birth, might be an entertaining topic at parties, but no policy bureaucrat would give the idea serious consideration. The *Archaic Record* was clear on the subject: "The Root-Races are neighbors and kin to one another, just as the Malkings are their lords and protectors. To extend one to the other without defending a condition of distinction would be a denial of the distinction and, therefore, an effacement of their innate differences and the essential dignity of the individual."

Dr. Frame hoped that, as the need for expansion in both the labor force and the consumer sector intensified, resistance to Rooter citizenship would weaken and backing policy reform would become a risk worth taking. One could argue that since Welfare Districts were a relatively new phenomena, and nothing like them had existed during the Age of History, a shift away from literal readings of the AR had already occurred. Frame could name numerous precedents to support an argument that the AR was no longer the primary authority for policy making, yet the position was impracticable as the Inner Circles never prioritized empirical evidence.

Most recently, his research had taken a turn back to the Age of Creation, becoming retrospective, even theopological, and unapologetically pro-Rooter. With his new book, to be titled, *Before the Ninth*, he planned an exegesis of a fragment from the *Archaic Record*: "...and only the Ninth had need of keeping," quoted in the *Marginalia*. He hoped to find the original text, but the indexing system of the AR made matching a phrase to its source difficult. Trial and error lent only so much to one's research. In recent visits, however, he'd been blessed with an intuitive sense of the system's logic, an approach he hoped could be hewn into a more concrete research methodology.

From these scanty means, he eventually located a closely related passage directly from the AR: "Of the nine Root-Races—the first shapeless, the second skinless, the third boneless, the fourth blind, the fifth deaf, the sixth speechless, the seventh mindless, the eighth soulless—only the Ninth was wholly formed." Although little more evidence about the fate of the first eight Root-Races came to light, he remained implacable for the simple reason that if there was a Ninth, eight others must have come before. The Ninth, of whom he was one, was whole and had *need of keeping*; whereas the others did not. To keep as possession? To keep alive? Perhaps both. What then happened to the other races? Extermination? Or did they still exist? Some held *the Ninth* referred to the Ninth Circle. Given the Kosmocratores' love of symbolism, layered meaning, and symmetry, the concurrence of the

Ninth Root-Race living within the Ninth Circle was no co-incidence. Rooters were born every day blind, deaf, or mute. His own sister was half-deaf. A belief that the phenomena was *an atavistic regression to honor the lost races* had found adherents amongst young mortals. Others believed the traits were proof that the other eight Root-Races walked amongst them to this day. Without proof or even much conviction, Frame believed this to be the most likely scenario.

The cloud now beyond view, Dr. Frame left the table for the stacks and retrieved the same two volumes as he had yesterday and a week ago, as last month and the month before, and back at the culling bower, he turned to the same two pages, reading over the same passages, thinking about probabilities and the power of the fragment in textual interpretation.

He saw Professor Wrengold in the First Annex of the *Marginalia* displaying a very peculiar behavior. The Professor—who Frame had never seen in the Library before noon—walked through the stacks with closed eyes, pulling a single, apparently random, volume from the stacks, and setting it on the circular center table. The Professor then exited the First Annex for the Second. Curious, Frame peaked around the hall doorway and watched Wrengold's shadow against the wall mime a repeat of the first action. Then moving into plain view, the Professor returned to the First Annex and set the book beside the first. Frame walked back to the culling bower and began rereading the very early volume of the *Archaic Record*, the Langer skin vellum waxy and brittle.

The Library furniture presented a problem as the design was meant to accommodate Malkings, not mortals. Frame always brought a folding chair from home and placed two mass-market editions of the *Marginalia* on the seat, which brought him up to a level where he could read an open text flat on the table. He chose to work at the culling bowers, as they were lower than the other tables in the Library. The rationale for this design plan completely eluded him, but he was grateful nonetheless.

Dr. Frame reached into his academy gown and retrieved a leather pouch from which he poured a handful of seeds onto the table. These he used for tabulation. Preliminary textual research was always accompanied by numerical data. In tandem they produced the means to extrapolate broader conclusions before the primary research was complete. Professor Wrengold was known for the assorted bean method and, of course, CSS, which the Professor adamantly denied, though it was common knowledge in the department. Frame observed the intensity of the denial was the biggest giveaway.

Freed-Rooters were taught by free-Rooter faculty, though nothing prevented Malkings from attending Rooter classes. In a class of forty, you could expect four or five, especially when the topic was Malking culture and politics. They simply never tired of hearing mortal descriptions of themselves. Occasionally, failing Malking students were given the choice between expulsion or passing a course taught by a Rooter. Some over-identified with Rooter culture and enrolled exclusively in classes from within the Rooter curriculum, ignoring the truth of their advisors' warning that no one in the Admin District would hire a Malking with a Rooter education.

Dr. Frame's high profile forecasting work for BRRAS put him in a unique position, as did the success of his recent book, *History Without Error, the Nuts and Bolts of Predictive Science*, all of which compelled the University to give him a class in the Malking sector. Dr. Frame considered the opportunity an honor, while experiencing an unsettling trepidation at the prospect. Malking students often adopted the post-adolescent personas of their Rooter peers. The irony that they'd been alive for more than twenty thousand global orbits was lost on them. Integrating Malkings into a class of mortals could be disrupted by the smallest oversight, if they failed to bring their own desk and chair for example.

In society at large, where freed-Rooters were ostensibly living amongst the Malkings with the rights and freedoms of real citizens, they were by and large still segregated. They were prohibited from using money and had no political voice, even on the level of neighborhood councils and petitions. Special kiosks were stocked with necessities identical to those distributed inside the Ninth Circle. On paper, BRRAS was not the controlling agency of the policy, since their mandate was the Ninth Circle. Jurisdiction had been given to the Bureau of Building and Trades, but they had no interest in any policing power beyond building inspection and were happy to let BRRAS run things off the books. The implementation of the freed-Rooter policy was accompanied by a short but robust publicity campaign promoting tolerance and stated the Lineal Descendant as well as the Bureaus of Enforcement and Well Being were to take a zero tolerance approach when it came to violations against freed-Rooters' civil rights. The campaign underscored the various accommodations in place designed to protect and serve freed-Rooters. "Where a difference in size might cause untold inconvenience for a friendly Rooter trying to shop in a store intended for Malkings, a store for each advances the mission of harmony, efficiency, and compassion."

Annually, according to the Welfare Amendment tagged onto Guardian Law, Rooters must attend at least one Freedom Fair to be held at the welfare stadium in each sector of the

79

Ninth Circle. There any interested Malking or freed-Rooter could claim a Ninth Circle Rooter of their choice. Once claimed, a Rooter could live within the Inner Circles, free to work menial jobs for a few extra chits. Until recently, claiming a Rooter was indistinguishable from enslaving a Rooter and was known as *slave-claiming*. Many reports of neglect and other forms of abuse were common. After the reforms introduced by the Lineal Descendant, *slave-claiming* was abolished. Consequently the phrase *to claim* was outlawed and replaced by *to free*. Rooters already *claimed* were *freed* and given the choice to remain in the inner circles or return to the Ninth. Forty percent remained and forty percent returned. Twenty percent exiled themselves to the Surroundings—beyond the Ninth Circle, beyond the Creation Grid—and/or they committed suicide. It was assumed that those who chose to live in the Surroundings lived amongst the lead slag left over from the Kosmocratores lead teeth, but no one really knew because no one returned from there, or no one said if they had. There were no records. In general, Malkings and Rooters shared the perception that nothing existed outside the Grid.

BRRAS identified several unwelcome consequences of abolishing *slave-claiming*. First, Malkings and freed-Rooters virtually ceased attending annual Freedom Fairs. The precipitous drop in attendance translated into a spiraling decline in the number of freed-Rooters. The last census of the Ninth Circle indicated that no more than five percent were leaving welfare districts annually. Forecasts from the Assembly were generally pessimistic about the trend, one Assemblier went so far as to say the situation was like a "cinched hose without pressure"; i.e., if fewer leave now, fewer still will leave in the future. Assembliers and Admin District analysts anticipated a negative impact on an economy buoyed by high growth in the bauble sector—growth largely due to the new consumer base created by the first wave of freed-Rooters. Subsidies made the bauble market inside the Blue Spires entirely unprofitable to all but a handful of manufacturers, and the recent burst of smaller, less staid (some might say less nepotistic) manufacturers was considered a healthy trend. Ironically, the most recent Admin projections indicated that by the next census, due to Imperial reforms, the rate of migration would drop further to three percent. According to the forecast, "The leadership becomes more unpredictable, less at ease, less convinced and less convincing." To his great frustration, Dr. Frame noted the most recent data as well as all reportage in the Paper omitted a crucial factor in their reports. At first glance it was curious that more freed-Rooters weren't freeing other Rooters at claiming fairs. Early attempts to do so had come up against unmovable impediment: a Rooter claimed by a freed-Rooter would not be allocated their own credits and must be supported from the charity of their sponsor. Finding himself in the unusual position of earning enough credit to support several others besides himself, he had offered to bring his family over; they, however, declined, stating they'd rather stay home. The more significant yet less discussed consequence was the economy benefitted from the influx if free labor freed-Rooters brought to the Grid.

Statistical forecasting was the domain of the Admin District and, more recently, the University. Dr. Frame was primarily a lecturer but had recently been brought in by BRRAS to help with their forecasting, in the hopes of counteracting the downward trends of Rooter migration. And while the work for BRRAS proved to be indispensable, he could not claim to be an employee of BRRAS, or any bureau of the Admin

District, because of laws prohibiting Rooters from working in exchange for payment. The University was much more forgiving in this regard, and while he was not paid for his research and lectures, his basic amenities were provided through government credits, while luxuries were paid for through the Barter Provision of the Root-Race Labor Law. His colleagues at the University had found a loophole: "The State shall sanction the exchange of one thing for another between agents of the Root-Race, given the aforementioned constraint on 'one thing' and 'another' to exclude money or resources upon which the value of money is determined, i.e., chits or credit. With regards to like-minded exchanges between willing agents of the Root-Race and the general citizenry or institutions, petitions may be filed with BRRAS." Ironically, the stigma of a Rooter working in the Admin District beyond the University and by extension the Library was so strong that BRRAS insisted Dr. Frame not file a petition for his work with the Bureau. Instead they paid him with money, which itself was odd as, generally, Malkings considered money a pinnacle of culture and one that distinguished them from Rooters. A further irony, Dr. Frame found the possession of money a huge inconvenience as it was entirely illegal for him to have or spend. Left with the options to either spend in the black market or hoard, he never developed an attachment to it or its value.

In the days leading up to teaching the all-Malking class, Dr. Frame had been warned by colleagues to expect a display of disturbing, even offensive, hijinks, manifesting from that narrow psychological spectrum adopted by Malkings to define themselves as college students. The pseudo-behavior included spit wad fights, langer imitations (a langer falling out of a tree, a langer eating its own feces, a langer defecating on another langer), Rooter imitations (a Rooter masturbating, a Rooter performing sexual intercourse, a Rooter eating food, a Rooter dying from various causes, natural and unnatural).

Thus, Frame approached the classroom with apprehension, repeating to himself, "I am walking with full composure and purpose in my stride." Malkings were obedient to authority; but they were also prone to outbursts and other expressions of impulsive behavior, which were amplified by peer pressure. He imagined his briefcase becoming a shield against spit wads, while he cut a path to the oversized podium, behind which he would hide until the tenor of the room became conducive to teaching. Frame opened the door. The class was orderly and attentive. He stood, caught off guard by the harmony of a room where he was dwarfed by the chairs, desks, and chalkboard, embraced by close odor of Malkings. Regaining his wits, he located an unused chair on which to stand and dragged it to the podium.

At 6:00 p.m. he watched the sun set from the chair facing the westward window of his apartment, disappearing into nothing. From inside the Ninth Circle housing blocs the sun always set behind the wall. He had grown up with that view. Now, living in Fourth Circle, a clear view of the wall would require a telescope. Yet the thought of it setting behind the wall remained the truth for him. He woke in the dark again, thinking, *Only the view has changed. Light always gives way to darkness, disappearing behind the wall.* He realized he'd fallen asleep in his chair. He remained sitting until the sun went back to setting, the light shrinking away so darkness could return. Neighboring apartments became visible as interior lights came on. The clock read 6:01 p.m. His secretary had called, her voice crisp and confident on the answering machine. Convincing the department to give him a Rooter secretary had been ridiculously difficult. "I told your students an urgent meeting at BRRAS required your canceling class. Please let me know if tomorrow you are again to meet with the bureau chief."

Living amongst Malkings had a way of diminishing the value of time, the preciousness of unrepeatable moments. Thus far, he'd been careful not to let too much of their immortality rub off on him (however much that was even possible), but how else could he explain sitting in his chair for twenty four hours doing absolutely nothing?

6

an open circle

i

the assembly

If the Lineal Descendant held power by divine right, the Assembly of Forecasters and Predictive Historians did so by divine knowledge. Without the Kosmocratores' mandate, it is said, the seat of the Lineal Descendant wouldn't last a minute past midnight; but, if the Assembly filled the seat, the Kosmocratores themselves couldn't stop their ascendancy. To ask if the Assembly is of the public, private, or Imperial sectors is to misunderstand their relationship to the rest of the Creation Grid. The Assembly is a self-policed, self-regulated organization that operates without any state funding. It is wholly protected from public and governmental scrutiny, and yet by law their work must be made available and entrusted to the public domain. The Assembliers oversee the way things are and the way things will be. They are shepherds of the truth and the future.

The secrets of Assembly are hidden in their methods of prediction. We can know them by what but not how they create. *Forecasts* are localized and narrow in focus. They embrace a relatively brief period of time, usually no more than one hundred years. They are created for various levels of state and local government to facilitate public policy-making. *Predictive histories* take a broader look over an extended period of time and are instrumental in controlling the public's understanding of past and future events.

Forecasts and predictive histories are composed following a manual called *The Predictive Pathmark*, passed on by the Kosmocratores to the First Assembly. The manual declares, *The measure of a prediction's truth is in its purity.* Consequently, Assembliers eschew all empirical data except the annual census reports produced by the Admin offices. Forecasts and predictive histories are derived from prior forecasts and predictive histories, beginning with the models first provided by the Kosmocratores. The dissemination of the future is carefully managed to produce the greatest positive effect on the present while minimizing the cost to its authors. This is called *the compromise of exclusive outcomes.*

Assembliers author two types of forecasts. *Projection forecasts* outline events pertaining to a single *prediction strand.* The complete forecast is made public on the day corresponding to the first day of the forecast. Depending on the demands of the inquiry, the report may be broken down into months, weeks, days, even minutes, and its scope never exceeds one year. (Exceptions do exist. Secretary Lamb's experimental text, *Two Years by Seconds*, predicts the movement of a dust mote from its creation, its transformation into a dust pile, and its eventual transfer to the dustbin. According to the forecast, Janitor Orl discovered the dust pile behind a futures vending machine and swept it onto a copy of *The Open Circle*. After discarding the dust, the janitor resumed setting up chairs for the community meeting to be held later that day. Why didn't Orl use a dustpan? This remains uncertain. It is known, however, that Orl was not gender curious, as might be supposed, the free weekly having been left by someone attending an earlier meeting. The forecast contains over sixty million individual entries and makes free use of *A Predictive History of Dust and other Particles* by Grand Assemblier Clay. While neither has any practicable value, and Clay in particular was the object of pointed criticism from particulate epidemiologists, both reports are important milestones demonstrating the almost limitless predictive capacity of the Assembly's methods.)

The second type, *One-to-one forecasts* (or *one-to-ones*), are so named because of the one to one ratio between event and prediction. They are created the prior year and released one day at a time according to the corresponding day of the forecast. Typically, institutional analysts and Admin Secretaries receive forecasts several months in advance of the public. Assembliers have found prejudicial release facilitates acceptable correspondence between a forecast and its *predictive threshold*. Once Admin Secretaries receive an advanced copy, they tend to implement policy that reflects the conditions outlined in the forecast, if for no other reason than provides a template to follow. Institutional analysts (primarily academics in the Predictive Sciences) will tend to evaluate a forecast as a construct, and full-scale critiques of the Assembly and its methods are not uncommon. The precept *neg = pos*, once controversial amongst Assembliers, states that prerelease discourse—positive *or* negative—give a forecast deeper roots in the public's shared consciousness. The strongest advocates of this position, mostly junior and restless mid-level Assembliers, say a critical response only makes their work more *lifelike*.

Predictive histories are composed hundreds, even thousands of years before the events they describe. Their scope, though, is equally broad, relying on existing forecasts, prior predictive histories, and census data relevant to the subject. Predictive histories function as a framework on which to hang forecasts. They are also a primary tool for teaching in the predictive sciences. New histories are published on a regular basis, often providing a point of departure in the wake of unsettling events. All predictive histories strive to be *directionally correct*, a concept related to *directional correctness* and *directional correction*. (Not to be confused with *directionally correct correction*, i.e., the correction of a directionally incorrect prediction intended to be correct.)

The relationship between forecasts, predictive histories and the Assembliers who create them is closely knit. The original nine Assembliers chosen by the Kosmocratores are now known as the First Assembly. With the exception of Assemblier Nole's censure and subsequent eternal institutionalization at the Grid's only mental hospital, the First Assembly remains unchanged. The senior forecasters rarely appear publicly, preferring the close confines of the Assembly building. The modest headquarters, built on a single lot with blocks cast from Palace slag, sits in humble contrast to the adjacent Admin building, occupying three lots and constructed in the old forum style, even boasting an early freeze depicting the nascent universe before the Age of Creation.

The Kosmocratores gave the original nine a mandate to add new Assembliers as circumstance demanded, and over the last twenty thousand years, the organization had grown to well over ten thousand members. The University's Predictive Science Department functioned as a recruiting and training ground for new staff. The money and other resources given by the Assembly to the University made it the biggest benefactor after the Offices of the Imperial Regent.

The methods of prediction have been so successful that many government and private organizations developed their own systems—much to the annoyance of an Assembly obsessive about controlling how and what information became public. When the Admin Offices implemented a method of statistical prediction, replacing a function once filled by the Assembly, they did so without soliciting the help of the Assembly, even bluntly refusing help when help was offered. An unpleasantness arose between the two, compelling the most senior members of each organization to abandon the custom of swapping offices on the anniversary of the Kosmocratores departure. The annual Rites of Humiliation, practiced for over a millennia, ceased entirely. While the tension was palpable, the two organizations did not neglect their directives to work for the betterment of the Inner Circles, the Imperial Regent and the Circle of Nine—working as they did at the pleasure of the Lineal Descendant. Assembliers limited their effort to that which was absolutely required or which was also in the self-interest of the Assembly. The Admin's refusal to reach out led the Assembly to further isolate itself from other high-echelon Grid bureaucracies.

The power of the Assembly is not simply the power of individuals or even the power of an institution. It is the power of a foundation upon which the edifice of society rests. Deep in the basement of the Financial District building, Investors spend their waking hours holed up in the claustrophobic confines of investment carrels. Commodities and other industry shares are traded, but it is the predictions and futures markets where the real capital is invested. The most common and least risky straight predictions trade on the outcome of Assembly forecasts, mainly projection forecasts, though one-to-ones and even predictive histories are traded as well. Value is determined by how closely a prediction corresponds with an actual outcome, creating additional pressure on policy makers to steer events towards a prediction. While the practice is discouraged, a trading market exists for negative outcomes as well, known pejoratively as the *null-to-void market*.

The prediction futures market trades on a wide range of unpredictables, from the percentage of accurate predictions of a given year to a prediction's actual content. Assembly Analysts maintain massive catalogs of fragments and strands for the sole purpose of facilitating investing. These are freely shared with senior Investors as they too greatly enhance the probability of a prediction's positive outcome.

The adage, *The further the future, the closer the profit or loss*, characterizes the high-risk, high-gain reality of long-term prediction futures.

ii

A Mortal History

As the predictive sciences gained wider application, and their existing application became more complex (causal factors included a field of reference that grew with each passing century and the strides made in *Archaic Record* hermeneutics), the Assembliers set about to publish a survey of past forecasts and predictive histories for use by the University as a resource of primary texts and commentaries. After an initial appraisal of possible topics, anomalies in the form of *vertical* and *horizontal coverage gaps* forced a halt to the project, and Archivists turned their attention to vetting their own work and locating sources for missing data. Despite the sheer volume of material, the task proved to be relatively easy as the gaps were restricted to the predictive work concerning beings below the Ninth Root-Race. A folder with the subject

90

heading *Mortal Beings Under R-r/9* contained a sheet of paper with the typed heading *A Natural History of Creation.* It was taped to a multi-paged document entitled *A Census of Species Indigenous to the Creation Grid.* Many Assembliers, especially those senior members with the most at stake, expressed enormous anxiety over missing zoological data. Their concern arose not from the gaps per se but from the failure to address the factors that made the gaps possible.

Just over twenty thousand years earlier, the Assembliers were hard at work learning their craft, performing the rote task of *predictive modeling,* and memorizing the numerical analogs of empirical data. All true predictive work was forbidden until the Age of History, making even a predictive history of their own creation impossible. While this quandary produced a mild befuddlement, the young Assembliers continued their work without interruption, demonstrating diligence and an unfailing devotion to the Creators. Several years passed with little change of routine, until one morning their Kosmocratore tutors arrived with a dozen carts of predictive documentation on the subject of immortal creation. They informed the Assembliers they had graduated and the documents were a gift to inaugurate the Assembly archive and the beginning of the Age of History.

Soon afterwards, the Kosmocratores issued the sacks of jelly that became the first generation of Root-Race mortals. Once the second generation had been issued by the mortals themselves, the Kosmocratores began the creation of lower beings. In what most Malkings considered an inexplicable digression, the Creators halted their work and delivered a memo to the Animal King population: "Urgent modification required. Please report to nearest Creation Center." And so each Animal King was endowed with a valence. They built the

Library of the *Archaic Record*, and then they were gone, shooting up through clouds and sky into the invisible cosmos. The Assembliers were left to sort out the inconsistencies between the *Archaic Record*'s account of the lower being population and the first census of mortal life inside the Creation Grid. The Kosmocratores' predictive work regarding lower beings was much grander than their actual accomplishments—an obvious conclusion, even without the census. Where the AK named thousand of beings, including hundreds of red-blooded creatures, the census recorded only two red-blooded creatures, with the preponderance of species falling under the heading *Blood Sucking Insects*. Thus any subsequent predictive history of the lower beings would contradict the scripture, sacred, incontrovertible, and wildly inaccurate.

To cope with the problem, First Assembliers began using phrases like *...double bind... ...impossible task... ... merely lower beings... ...who are we to contradict the wishes of our creators....* . Others were more critical claiming the history could have been written during the twenty years that lapsed from the beginning of history to the creation of the lower beings, and Animal Kings had access to just the first volume of the *Archaic Record*. How, asked their peers, could a predictive history suppose mortality as a contingency when Animal Kings had no concept of mortality? Granted, they witnessed the creation of the Ninth Root-Race, but the anomaly of their being small and growing little bigger revealed nothing about mortality per se. Predictive science, if it could be generalized at all, was the art of arranging known factors, and in this instance the Assembliers had almost nothing from which to work. Ah yes, replied others, but the strength of predictive science was its ability to handle the most unexpected contingencies.

In any case, no Assemblier wrote a predictive history of the lower beings. Assemblier Nole may have been an exception, but the Kosmocratores had banished Nole from the Assembly for composing a predictive history before the beginning of history. That was the official charge, but rumors continued to circulate that Nole's history concerned the creation of lower beings. Many newer Assembliers believed a predictive history really did exist, buried in the archives somewhere. When *A Natural History of Creation* surfaced, hopes were aroused even though the document contained only a five-word title.

All filed archives were permanent. All files were required to include a title and the corresponding document. An archive missing one or both of these items placed the Assembly in breach of custody and means of procurement. If the work had been written and was now lost, it would have to be found. If no such document existed, it would have to be written—despite the fact that no history had ever been written a posteriori. And though a predictive history from the present point forward would exclude the *creation* of the lower beings and the first twenty thousand years of their existence, it would close a rather conspicuous gap at the other end. In addition to finding any documents that may have been lost, the Assembliers instructed Senior Archivist Hurley to locate all material concerning the lower beings beneath the Root-Race. No one said so out loud, but there was a shared sense that even the best possible outcome would be little more than damage control.

If a missing document was found one could verify the existence of the document, but if a missing document was never found, one could never say with complete certainty that it did or did not exist. The sheer quantity of material made absolute verification impossible. Twenty thousand years of histories and predictions were filed in archive boxes and stored in three climate-controlled warehouses directly below the public square (once the basement to the Palace of the LD) around which the Assembly building and thirty other central government and social service buildings were built. Archivists accessed documents using a massive semi-automated retrieval system. One merely dialed in an archive box index number and the requested material was delivered to a designated loading dock via an intricate belt and pulley system.

Over one thousand workers in the employ of the Assembly managed the underground operation. Five thousand years ago, the trade guilds had made an appeal to the authority vested in the Circle of Nine, claiming the retrieval system should be run by guild workers under the auspices of the Department of Machine Maintenance and Engineering, especially as DOMME—in tandem with the United Assemblers Union—had designed, fabricated, and assembled the apparatus. On paper, DOMME was a government branch; in practice, it was lobbying body that secured government contracts on behalf of the Trade Guild Alliance.

iii

The Trial

The trial lasted a single day and was held in the grand courtroom over which the Circle of Nine presided. The plaintiffs had two attorneys, one representing DOMME and the other TGA; both wore the requisite black court smocks, which tied around their naked backs like a smelter's apron. A box handler from Building Maintenance and Development named Grohl sat between the two attorneys. The decision to bring Grohl was a rhetorical flourish concocted by the plaintiffs' legal team to illustrate who would most be impacted if the Circle of Nine did not intervene on behalf of the trade guilds. Grohl's body was oiled. The attorneys had been quite insistent on this point: "Look Grohl, there's really no room for negotiation. You must be naked, shaved and oiled. Yes, oiled." Grohl was timid, uncomfortable in public, and quite used to wearing a box handler's short-dress. Ultimately, the selection process had had only one consideration: size—and Grohl was easily the biggest Guild worker on the Grid. Temperament had not been a consideration, and consequently, they were stuck with a trembling yet very glistening edifice named Grohl.

The chairs on the defense side were empty. Earlier an Assembly attendant had arrived carrying a *for external-use only* presentation box containing twelve mimeographed copies of a document, ostensibly meant to act in lieu of an attorney. Disregarding any relevant protocol, the attendant read the cover letter aloud before exiting without further address: "The archives represent the total work of the Assembly since the beginning of history. Given its designation as a First Echelon Institution by the Kosmocratores, the Assembly is protected from public and governmental scrutiny regardless of circumstance. As evidence supporting the unerroneousness of this claim, underscoring the purposelessness of the plaintiff's suit, and demonstrating its overall variance with Creation Grid protocols, the First Assembly submits for evidence a special predictive history of the trial about to commence. Drawn from the precedent of First Echelon, cited above, the report concludes a unanimous ruling against the plaintiff."

The Circle of Nine were invisible. Popular understanding had it that the Circle of Nine was visible only to itself and the Lineal Descendant. Many concluded from this tenuous assertion that the Circle of Nine was not, in fact, invisible; rather, it was they, the public, who were blind. In any case, the invisibility was a distraction in court, as no one knew where to look. Even with nine chairs lined up in a row facing the defendants, plaintiffs, attorneys, witnesses, experts, clerks, et cetera, the attendees were left gazing in the general direction of the court without a common focus. To those being regarded, the behavior was just as disconcerting. Over the years, the Circle of Nine had attempted a number of fixes that failed to end in any measurable improvement. During the early days of the court, they constructed nine cut-out figures and painted each in their own likeness, placing one behind each of their nine chairs. The effort only intensified the court's uneasiness. For a short period, they donned the off-white robes worn by inner-circle administrators, but once again, the attempt backfired. The animate robes without hands, heads, or feet caused an instinctual panic response, and anyone entering the courtroom quickly fled at first sight of the hollow robes. More recently, they had arranged the entire court in a circle, hoping to affect a greater judicial intimacy, wherein their awful difference might be more palatable to the public. Unfortunately, the close proximity to nine invisible judges produced a paralyzing fear, crippling even the most well-rehearsed actions of the court. After each of these attempts, the Circle of Nine found themselves with an empty docket until they promised through a flurry of memos that no more surprises awaited the public. In the end, the Circle of Nine mounted a single, pulsing, red light onto the bench. While the gazes were no more accurate, their uniformity lent the courtroom a welcome cohesion.

The Attorneys for the plaintiff argued that protection by the Imperial branch was only legitimate if the recipient was a true government organization. The Assembly's status being neither public, private, nor governmental was outside the writ of Imperial law and not in the interest of the body politic. Privately, trade guilds saw the trial as an opportunity to wedge the Assembly between two choices: 1) maintain privacy but give up special status and become another office of the government or 2) keep their special status but give up privacy and let outside workers run the retrieval system. They calculated that if the Circle of Nine found in favor of the plaintiff, the privilege of privacy would win out over autonomy. By law, such an outcome would mean the trade guilds had lost the civil suit and would not assume authority over the retrieval system. But by declaring the Assembly an office of the government, bound to the jurisdiction of Imperial law, the Assembly would lose the protection that had given them total impunity for the last fifteen thousand years. The trade guilds would then be in a position to further erode the Assembly's power with a campaign of litigation. Looking towards the big picture, the guilds considered their initial suit a single step towards the projected goal of winning the contract to run the underground warehouses. Once inside, they could make strategic use their strike prerogative.

But such thinking underestimated the influence of the Assembly. Very soon the hearing would be over, and with the barest effort they would walk away victors. When the court returned after a short recess, an Assemblier, accompanied by a single attendant, stood behind the table for the defense. The defendant wore a gray, hooded robe with the signature purple sash of the First Assembly. A face was not visible past the drawn hood, and except for an occasional trembling wheeze, the Assemblier stood motionless, indicating not the slightest recognition of the plaintiffs, then, making a quarter turn to face the pulsing, red light, began the formal address of obedience.

"By the Kosmocratores mercy, by their lead teeth, by their unfolding love, by their boundless embrace of all that is and all that is not, by our humble devotion to the Creators on high, by our awe of the Lineal Descendent and the wealth visited us by the benevolence of the Imperial Palace, by my submission before the Circle of Nine, who draw the rules of law from the *Archaic Record*, like water from a well, I aver my deposition to be one with the truth, upon the First Parthenogenone, the only miracle, the cosmic spool. Seek no further and you shall know."

The court echoed in whispered chorus, *Seek no further and you shall know.*

The red light pulsed.

"To the honorable First Circle and members of the court, I acknowledge the validity of the plaintiff's charge, and from one citizen to another I gladly recommend that the contract go to DOMME. Who better qualified to run the retrieval system than its engineers and machinists? Nor do I hold any doubt that precedent favors their side—"

The Assemblier bent over in a fit of tortured, mute choking, and the closing comments fizzled out mid-sentence. The attendant abandoned the whisker cart and scuttled over to help.

Amongst the many ways of determining seniority at the Assembly, the most ingrained was the beard. Animal Kings were hirsute compared to downy-haired mortals. As Animal King fashions often emerged as perverse mimes of the most basic and inescapable conditions of Root-Race's mortal existence, shaving, eating, sleeping, and adopting gender affects had been popular for millennia. Assembliers were resolute in never bending to the sways of popular opinion. Those who had been growing their beards for at least ten thousand years employed a whisker cart, similar to a garden hose reel mounted on a wheeled tripod, onto which the great length of hair was wound. Others preferred the bale and harness technique, in which the beard, tightly rolled up on itself, formed a round disk about one meter in diameter. The disk, or bale, was then fastened against the bearer's back by means of a harness. The bearer might be the owner of the beard or an Assembly intern recently elevated to custodis statua. Attendants were given many duties, but most spent their first few centuries as bearers, carrying a bale and harness or pushing a whisker cart.

"Unhand me! Back to your station!" cried the Assemblier to the attendant. "How dare you! It's effrontery! You'll be damned! Carbuncle! Scabrous clam! Enzyme-deficient weed! Licentious bean paste soaked in the urine of a thousand Rooters! Faulty chart!"

Releasing the venom had a visibly calming effect, and once the attendant had scrambled back to the cart, the Assemblier proceeded without interruption.

"A thousand apologies my lords. Assemblier Cleave at your service."

Executing a series of short bows and regaining focus on the pulsing red light the defense continued unimpeded.

"I recall the day when first we began our tenure as guardians of the mortals. During our training, the Creators provided workshops, seminars, and tutorials. Our preparedness was important as they entrusted us with dominion over the Grid. The time came for the Kosmocratores to leave, and we will forever be alive within their absence. Of course it's never that simple. In following out their instructions to build a unified Creation Grid, we remain always in their presence. The success of our work is not a testament of our accomplishment but of theirs. Without their hand we'd be nothing more than mortals who could not die! Recall the Kosmocratores' last words: *We leave you the way.*"

Again, in near unison, the court whispered, *Seek no further and you shall know.*

"The Creators will know more of our work than we can of theirs or even of our own."

Cleave produced a pair of half-round reading spectacles, which disappeared into the cowl of the Assemblier's robe. Reaching under the table, Cleave produced the standard pew edition of the *Abbreviated Marginalia*, a stock item in every municipal office. The plaintiffs did likewise with an ease of habit.

"I direct you to 'Book Two, Lectures on the Supreme Order', Chapter Two, 'Within the Invisible: A Case for Secrecy in the Upper Echelons'. Please bear with me as I read the entire lesson. In some it will spark fond reminiscences…" Looking directly at the plaintiffs for the first time, Cleave added, "…in others less fond.

"'What follows invisibility?' the Kosmocratores ask. 'With our guidance you will form a hierarchical, sociopolitical infrastructure upon which a unifying bureaucracy can flourish. Consider this effort a part of a continuum beginning with creation and ending with its end. The continuum is littered with significant events. Relevant to the moment, we can cite each as our own creation by the Impersonal Deity; your creation by us; the creation of the Root-Race (more will be said on this subject nearer the time of their inception); and the creation of a social fabric that will endure as you must endure. Your immortality made the formula for this fabric a challenge. I'm not giving anything away when I tell you, eternity is a very long time.

"'There are obstacles. As immortal as you are, you must suffer the burden of life, the life of the living. Where we came from the lifeless dust and vapor, you are made of flesh stuff. Experience teaches that all living beings, mortal and immortal, embody many frailties. You perceive a division between yourself and others, between yourself and the world, between yourself and your Creators, even between yourself and yourself. These divisions sabotage Unity and create the necessity for Law to mediate the divides. Thus, you must endure our persistent iteration that Law is the antitheses of Unity, just as it functions in the stead of Unity. Through Law you see a way towards Unity, but let the record be clear: You cannot reach for Unity, for Law moves you still further from its radiance. Law is a divider corresponding to the divisions within. Once your being is split by twos, it knows the world as a complex of opposing asmods: the thing and its opposite, the beginning and the end, Agonie and grace, ocular science and blindness. Blame is in part ours. With immortality, we assumed, you'd overcome a life of divisions, what we call *the life of too many faces*. Still, we hope you recognize immortality is incompatible with division. Later, once you've mastered the Guardian's technique, you will meet a race of mortal beings gifted with language and ingenuity. Through them you'll see division is more suited to them than you.

"'By charting your epistemic topology, we formed the working hypothesis that a weak aspect can be countered by a strong one. Following then, we balanced depravity with systematic thinking, something at which you excel. Your knowledge beyond knowledge is myopic, yet you have an aptitude for organization and analysis. The question for us, then, was how much should you know? We began a series of experiments. Three groups were chosen at random and given different degrees of knowledge. Group A = Total Knowledge; Group B = No Knowledge; and Group C, the control, = Knowledge As Created. The three groups were then asked to describe the origin of that which is. We were less interested in their descriptions than their states of mind in the aftermath. In the opinion of three independent clinician groups, A and B showed a similar mixture of clinical depression and anxiety. Predictably the control group's response was both less extreme and more diverse. Our clinicians used the following descriptors for group C: sleepy, nonplussed, bored, annoyed, jubilant, then sad, red-colored, angry, non-responsive, itchy, emboldened, uncertain, skeptical, critical, jealous, paranoid, limpid, dry, tearful and violent, powdery, nice, antagonizing, moist, confident, greenish, sociable, coercive, lackadaisical, agreeable, guileless, sentimental, blasé, uncompromising, lewd, courteous, cavalier.

"'A second experiment evaluated knowledge production and its effects, with an emphasis on native conditions. A large, random sampling was made from the general population. The group attended a series of workshops in which a few of the more abstruse aspects of cosmology were revealed to them. Upon completion, the group reintegrated into the general population and was encouraged to discuss their experiences with other members of their community. At this point, we were most interested in the reactions to the groups' testimony. These can be organized into three categories: 1) incredulity; 2) uncritical acceptance; 3) critical consideration. Once the subjects exhausted the new but incomplete knowledge, they

102

were ill-equipped to provide anything but conjecture to convince, disabuse and/or inform their audience. None of the subjects acknowledged a limit to their knowledge, presumably because the workshop experience had instilled a sense of distinction that separated them from their peers, making honest concession difficult. Where total knowledge and total absence of knowledge had produced clinical depression and anxiety, exposure to partial knowledge and conjecture produced more favorable results. With few exceptions, those in the three response categories—incredulity; uncritical acceptance; critical consideration—entered a state of mild to severe befuddlement when those the in study group imparted both what they knew and what they did not. Moreover, the study group itself experienced a similar state of befuddlement once they had overextended themselves and their short-lived power of influence evaporated due to a knowledge deficit.

"'From these studies we isolated two tendencies, curiosity and indifference, which in addition to depravity, required containment. Together the three are known as the *master drive triangulate*, a concept now closely tied to the study of Animal King psychodynamics. Finally, then, we concluded the Creation Grid would not survive without containing the MDT. Discovering the efficacy of befuddlement as an MDT damper suggested an elegant solution to the problem.

"'Once we are gone, you will be responsible for administration and policy-making; you will be responsible for the development of the governing bureaucracy. You will be responsible for the welfare of the Root-Race. Most importantly you will be responsible for the development of a hermeneutics of the *Archaic Record*. The results will be called a *History of Last Lessons* and will have two parts. The first will contain the record of your encounter with us, your Creators, the

Kosmocratores. The second will contain interpretive studies of the *Archaic Record* and events the Circle of Nine deems relevant. It will never be complete and will always need updating. Only the upper echelons will know the *History of Last Lessons*.

"'The *Archaic Record* contains truths on every topic, from customs to technology. It is written in a difficult hand, and you will have to fill many pages of the History to reveal its answers. This will be your primary and most enduring encounter with befuddlement. The second is called *dissemination*, wherein the truth shall be given a life in the world. You must disseminate truth and befuddlement in equal measure.

"'After our departure, you will come to know the Assembly of Forecasters and Predictive Historians. As they produce knowledge, they will also produce mystery. Knowledge and mystery; together they are the terms of befuddlement. The Assembliers, as you will know them, must be free to shift between worlds. They must be the floating eye; the untouched thief; the impossible Agonie. Mystery has no final point. Mystery never arrives, never becomes knowing. All mysteries remain half of what they are, the rest slip back into obscurity.'"

Upon finishing the passage, a bell rang and the red light turned green, signaling judgment for the defense.

iv

Hig

The job of recovering extant predictive material pertaining to lower beings was given to three junior Archivists, Hig, Harley, and Jewel. They were close to earning their degrees in Predictive Science and knew working as Archival Interns was the surest way to secure a job at the Assembly. The choice of Hig surprised no one, as he had already demonstrated considerable leadership and talent as a researcher. Harley and Jewel were on probation for their less-than-stellar performances and had been assigned to Hig for the *great influence wrought by a sterling character upon those still veined with dross.* Or so the University liaison had successfully argued.

The work of an Archivist was laborious. Projects were divided into three stages—*proposal, composition, enactment*—and each stage required approval by the First Assembly to move forward. Roughly ninety percent of all projects were authored by Assembliers; the remaining ten percent being split between Archivists and Assemblier Interns—or in the present case, Archivist interns. Most research material went to Assembliers preparing proposals or—having already gained approval—composing *Forecasts* and *Predictive Histories.*

A Natural History of Creation was unprecedented for two reasons. First, the choice of author. The strict hierarchy within the Assembly placed Assembliers above Archivists, even junior Assembliers were considered more distinguished than senior Archivists. Building Maintenance and Development workers were handled by a separate hierarchy established by the trade guilds, which had no role in the Assembly's business, even though the strike prerogative gave guilds considerable power of negotiation. Assemblier interns had no authority over Archivists; however, as each Intern had an Assemblier sponsor, interns gained their sponsor's authority by proxy. Archive interns had no sponsors and entered the Assembly under the broad designation *new intern*.

Hig surmised the appointment of three Archivist interns to a job normally handled by senior Assembliers reflected more the status of the project than a shift of policy regarding Archivist interns. The temporal framework of the history, one which started at the end and moved towards the beginning, had likely sent an anxious shiver through the ranks of Assembliers who feared a back-looking history to be not only counterintuitive but possibly even blasphemous. Not to mention, with Archive interns at the helm, the project could easily be squashed or discredited without embarrassment to the senior Assembliers.

Hig began with the *Census Inventory of Species*, creating a bibliography of possible sources and an index of important zoological terms. Once a citation to an existing archive was found, Harley and Jewel would retrieve the document from the archive warehouses, known amongst archivists as the *Cold Storage*: twenty thousand years of predictions, histories, and supporting material filed away in wooden archive boxes. The three interns spent most of their time in the culling bower, a room uniquely equipped for the sorting of archive material. A stairway led from the room down to a circular landing that housed the retrieval terminal for each warehouse. The First Assembliers had private access to the archive stacks from their chambers; the stairways built off main hallways serviced multiple floors and gave authorized personnel plebeian access to the stacks.

The culling bower adjoined the Research Supplies Office by a counter through which material was checked out and returned. The RSO was under the control of the DMD but functionally was much closer to Archives. Typically, Assembly staff developed the closest relationship to Suppliers over all other union workers. Indeed, it may be said suppliers had more in common with the Assembly staff than their fellow guild members.

The bower was large and open, allowing for free movement around a single, rectangular table. Hundreds of archive boxes were stored against the walls along the length of the table. The Acquisitions and Retrievals counter—where Assembliers checked out and returned archive material—and the Research Supplies Office were across from one another at the room's midpoint. To access the Tertiary File Annex one had to first pass Archivist Hurley's desk, and given the latter's unwelcoming disposition, few did. Most used the hallway entrance instead or avoided the annex altogether.

To obtain archived material, an Assemblier submitted an acquisition form at the Acquisitions and Retrievals counter. An Archivist then retrieved the relevant Archive boxes from the warehouses. Typically, a box contained material other than what had been requested. The Archivist's job, then, was to locate the specific documents requested and transfer them from the box to the smaller presentation box, which was placed on the counter along with a mimeographed copy of the acquisition form. At this point Archivists usually referred to the archive box as a *dummy box* as it remained stacked with the others in the culling room until the acquisitioned material was returned.

According to the *Archivist Code Manual* regarding box specifications, two presentation boxes must fit snugly inside a single archive box; further, a correct two-boxes-in-one-box configuration must result in five interior sides of an archive box (A) contacting four exterior sides of each presentation box (B, C). The code did not, however, specify the dimensions of either kind of box, leading to variations between boxes depending on the manufacturer. Realizing that without a master box regulating box dimensions the code would be violated, the First Assembliers held a closed-door conference with the four factories responsible for Assembly-box production. The action occurred just under fifteen thousand years ago. At this point in time, the trade guilds were highly regarded by the Creation Grid public. Whereas, the Assembly, by its very secrecy, was viewed as untrustworthy and isolationist. Thus, during the first epochs, the trade guilds were more influential than the Assembly. The guild reps from the four box manufacturers refused the Assembliers' request to standardize box dimensions, pointing to the existing contracts that made no mention of dimension and which would be binding until the end of eternity. After arduous negotiations on both sides, it was agreed that each of the four manufacturers would standardize their own boxes but no universal standard would be set. The guilds agreed as well to build presentation boxes in a proportion that conformed to the box code's two-in-one-box configuration for their own product. The archivists were left to sort out the actual logistics of integrating the four box designs. A product name had to be easily visible from the outside, so archivists could identify them by kind. These were the *Bilger Box*, *Creation Grid's Favorite*, *Rite Size*, and *From a Tiny Acorn*. When Harley and Jewel fetched material from the warehouses, they had to know which box would be used before requesting presentation boxes from the RSO. If an acquisition request required material from more than one archive box, separate presentation boxes had to be used unless both archive boxes were from the same manufacturer. No archivist could afford to dwell on the irony that no circumstance ever required a presentation box to be placed inside an archive box.

A poster on the door leading to the warehouses—yellow, skewed sideways, and hanging by a single tack—spelled out proper box protocol with a simple cartoon. A naked and hairless Animal King pointed to a chalkboard and a series of simple line drawings. Balloon one: 'Let's imagine that Archivist X has retrieved material for Presenter Y from archive boxes A, B, and C.' Balloon two: 'The Archivist will organize the material into the three corresponding presentation boxes i, ii, iii.' Balloon three: 'Remember to match each presentation box to a like archive box. In this illustration, Charlie the Archivist has a Bilger archive box, from which he transfers the acquisition into two Bilger presentation boxes.' Balloon four: 'Double check the pick up time written on the upper left-hand corner of the retrieval form.' Balloon five: 'After the material is checked in carefully re-file it into the corresponding archive box.' Balloon five: 'The empty presentation box is promptly returned to the Research Supplies Office.'

Archive boxes were static since their content never changed, and as stipulated in the *Assemblier Rules of Index, Retrieval & Preservation*, they were always returned to the same location. Whereas, presentation boxes were in flux, used over and over, filled with varying content for varying purposes, and ultimately returned empty to storage.

Hig, Harley, and Jewel struggled to find material regarding lower beings. Once the retrieval process was over, they had culled through over five hundred archive boxes. The relevant material fit easily into a single presentation box. Clearly there was not enough for an exhaustive work like *A Natural History of Creation.* Furthermore, what they did find was authored by the First Assembly, creating two obstacles. First, the examples were far from the senior Assembliers' finer moments; second, the research committee to which they had to report was also the First Assembly. There was serious concern amongst the junior Archivists of embarrassment for everyone involved.

Two days before the meeting, they sought consultation with their mentor, Archivist Hurley, who they found tucked away in the Tertiary File Annex, *Phenomenology-Pheromone.* The annex was plagued with dust from crumbling daubing and the absence of a janitor who had vanished without replacement three years ago. Hurley took enormous pride in personally dusting the files each week. As one of the most senior second-generation members, the station of Assemblier had been offered many times but Hurley always refused, insisting on remaining an Archivist.

Hurley, who had been at the Assembly for fifteen thousand years and nearly matched the First Assembliers in beard length, chose the less-complex bale method and a modest harness of threadbare jute. Many times they'd discussed the idea of purchasing a new harness but concluded each time that it would be rejected. Hig, Harley, and Jewel, now saddled with the impossible task of saving the First Assembliers from themselves, understood why Hurley had resolved to remain an Archivist.

As expected, Hurley was dusting files, hunched from the weight of the beard and the eons of dusting and filing.

They spelled out their predicament, as Hurley ushered them to sit on any one of several piles of overfilled folders cluttering the narrow lane between stacks.

"That's a pretty big pickle," said Hurley.

"A real pickle," echoed Jewel.

Hurley tore off the corner of a file folder and used the edge to dislodge a bit of tobacco between molars. "Look lads, you're not viewing the problem from the most advantageous angle. You're agitated by how it might affect you; that is, you're worried about a disaster jeopardizing your chances at becoming Archivists. Look at it from over here instead," gesturing to a seemingly random part of the room. "Start by thinking how someone else will be affected, regardless of your ambitions. From that point, maybe you can slowly turn it back towards yourselves. Only then will the disaster become a blessing not a curse." Hurley dropped the folder corner and struck a match on the No Smoking sign, "No Smoking" long since obscured by countless match strikes, lighting an enormous gourd calabash retrieved from within the folds of the Senior Archivist's dark-red cloak.

Obviously the risk that Hurley would start a fire was always high, and the three junior archivists hesitated before nodding politely to exit. They knew once the pipe was lit the conversation was over.

"Did you get any of that?" asked Harley.

"Not a pip," said Jewel.

"Let's give it some reflection and reconvene tomorrow morning," said Hig.

"I'm up on the second part, but don't count on me for the other. Hurley's a thorny chestnut that's for sure," said Jewel.

"Same here," added Harley.

"Okay, I'll do the reflecting if you both promise to get plenty of rest—we need to be in fine fettle tomorrow."

They met in the culling bower early the next morning. Hurley had left them a note scrawled on a sealed folder labeled Prehistory: "Have fallen victim to bad case of 'chaffing rash'.

111

May be the dust, may be the smoke, may be the embers in the Assembly." Harley and Jewel looked to Hig for an interpretation. Hig knew the single quotes indicated *chaffing rash* had a double meaning. If the *smoke* alluded to Hurley's advice, then *embers* referred to their presentation and *the dust* must be what they had stirred up or uncovered. Why be absent on this day? To avoid an association with the Archive Interns? Hurley was no coward. More likely, the absence gave them no option but to carry through with the meeting.

Meanwhile, Harley and Jewel shared a sinking feeling that their days at the Assembly were over. Hig, the most precocious, some would say reckless, of the three, laid out a plan that promised no harm to the others if it failed and triumph for all three if it succeeded. The culling bower felt empty without Hurley. One would be hard-pressed to explain such a feeling as the room was filled floor to ceiling with archive boxes.

"I need both of you to help with two things, then the rest is on me."

"Sure."

"Yeah, sure Hig."

"Once we're inside, I'm going to set the box on the table and wait—"

"You're what?" Harley interrupted.

"No way, Hig. That ain't for me."

"They'll hang us by the shorthairs."

"Or staple our hands together."

"You'll be the *Ninth* for sure."

"Trust me. We're going to be fine."

Hig had an unusually high valence, and Harley and Jewel believed even the committee would have a hard time resisting its persuasive power. The assumption went a long ways to assuage their anxiety, at least enough for them to move forward with a plan they feared and didn't understand. Both were mid-valence: pastel colors with little translucence, and animal aspects with vague definition and no dimension. Their colors and aspects shifted slowly, appearing sluggish compared to Hig's, whose prismatic colors revealed a full spectrum in every fragment and whose animal aspects were clear, animate, and present, as if the animals they represented actually existed in the world.

"Okay. Okay," said Harley.

"Jewel?"

"Yeah, okay. We'll do it."

"Once I set down the box, allow for the lapse of protocol to take hold, and when the silence becomes uncomfortable, that's when you begin sobbing like a baby Rooters with the colic."

"Just like that?" Jewel asked.

"It won't be hard," said Harley.

"With tears?"

"Tears would be fantastic."

Jewel asked, "Is that it?," sounding both hopeful *and* doubtful.

"No," replied Hig, "but the last part will be easy. The silence will be broken with a question regarding my name and station. I'll say, 'Archivist Intern Hig'. To which they'll say something derogatory. This is your cue to exit the room before they ask names. Walk out backwards, apologizing."

"What if they ask our names before yours?" asked Jewel.

"I'm the one that's broken protocol. But if they do, use that as the exit cue."

"If they ask, we leave."

"Right."

"You'll be hung by the shorthairs."

"If they've mine before I have theirs."

"I only hope you've sorted out all the angles," Harley said, tossing a crumpled piece of carbon paper into the culling bower waste bin.

v

The Assembliers

The committee sat on one side of a long oval table facing the door and the interns. All was darkness inside their hooded cloaks. Assemblier Branch sat in the middle with four colleagues on either side. The three junior archivists entered the Research Committee meeting room with an air of reluctance, and from what the committee could see, the work had not gone well. A research meeting might entail as many as eleven archivists, each with a cart, and each cart loaded with six boxes of spirit copies and mimeographs. Standard protocol required the archivists to form a line midway between the entrance and the table. Standing on the left side of their carts, they would wait until addressed by the Committee Chair. Typically, discussion carried on for some time before acknowledging the archivists, and this instance was no exception.

Flanked on either side by two fidgeting, trembling, empty-handed archivists, the third stood cartless yet unwavering, holding a single archive box. The Assembliers practiced what they called the *temporal enforcement of station* by ignoring the archivists to chat amongst themselves until no doubt remained regarding the hierarchy of authority to which all parties must conform. The one holding the box let out a pregnant sigh then without a *grant of permission* stepped forward

114

to set it on the table, squarely in front of Committee Chair
Branch. Presenting without a cart was rare though not without precedent. But an archive intern acting without a grant
of permission? That *was* unprecedented. The committee fell
into stunned silence. And while the room positively congealed
with tension, the other two archivists fell to their knees weeping. Nearly a minute passed before the Assembliers regained
their composure enough to continue. What of the third intern? There was no weeping or other outward sign of distress,
just the opposite, in fact, as if relinquishing the box had been
an act of liberation. The Assembliers checked one another's
hoods, then turned their collective attention to the eccentric
intern.

They nodded to give the Chair first prerogative to speak.

"Come now," said Branch. "A full scholarship to the University, and you bring us a box of scraps? This task is file
keeping compared to what awaits you after graduation. Or
maybe you're aiming for something in the Admin District.
The revocation of your visitor's pass is waiting."

"Quite so," said Assemblier Kone. The others now perked
up. "Did Hurley sign off on this?" asked Kone. "Been out with
a bit of the chaffing rash if I'm not mistaken." The table offered nods and uttered affirmations. "You," Kone said to the
standing intern. "What's you're name?"

"Archivist Hig, Assemblier Kone."

"Not an Archivist yet, I dare say," said Kone with raised
eyebrows. The other two interns scuttled backwards apologizing and fled out the door. The committee members broke
into laughter.

"Nor are *they*, my goodness."

"Jolly, jolly."

"They ran like fish."

"Yes, like fauns."

"Like fauns; they ran like fish and fauns."

"Well Hig," continued Kone. "It looks like they left you holding the box!" Kone shuffled a small pile of papers and coughed. "Now. Let's have a look at your manifest."

Hig stood, unwavering, with resplendent valences.

"Your Honor, if I may," began Hig. "The manifest is clipped to the front of the top folder, as per archive protocol."

Assemblier Cleave, on Branch's left, reached into the box and retrieved the first folder, handing it to Branch, who handed it to Kone, on Branch's right.

"Based on what we've already seen, forging Archivist Hurley's signature isn't beyond your conniving. Let's just have a look-see," said Kone. The Assemblier's hooded head slowly tilted left and then right, each time pausing as if recuperating from the effort. On its return to an upright position, Kone's head remained a few degrees shy of vertical. "Lamb, take a look at this," said Kone.

The paper was handed back to Branch and Cleave, then made its way to the far end of the table. Lamb opened the gray box that housed the Senior Authenticator's magnifying glass. As Lamb hunched over the magnified paper, the outer edge of a green-tinted visor became visible past the cowl. While the Authenticator methodically studied for traces of malfeasance, committee decorum became less disciplined. Sore and Lovely carved obscenities into the tabletop with thick, yellow prosthetic fingernails, manufactured from langer claws. Cleave's hood was down. Skittish laughter at the exposed, invisible head continued until Cleave replaced the hood, securing it with the sash from the Assemblier's robe, tied tight under the chin.

"Everything appears to be in order," announced Lamb.

Assemblier Kilhn, to Lamb's right, commandeered the manifest by dragging it across the table pinned beneath an invisible finger "Let's just see what we have here."

"If it pleases your Honor," said Hig.

Kilhn began to read the manifest, "'Item One: The Shifting Breeding Zones of the Gray-Winged Mosquito.' Am I to presume this accounts for the bulk of your archive?"

Kilhn paused. Hig nodded.

"'Item Two.' You've written, quote, 'Miscellaneous texts on the langer', end quote. This is an extraordinary bit of summary Hig; you've dismissed what may be the only relevant part of this archive." And here, Kilhn held up the paper for the Assembliers see. "A note at the bottom reads, 'Probably of no predictive value', end quote. Pray tell, are junior archivists now overseeing predictive hermeneutics? You really must keep us up-to-date on these things. Please, for our own edification, tell the committee."

"I apologize for any confusion resulting from my inexperience. I assure the members of the esteemed First Assembly that I have no intention of overstepping my station."

"I thought perhaps the times had changed without our knowing."

Scattered laughter and an extended gurgle interrupted Kilhn's interview. Sore and Lovely fell backwards in their chairs.

"So, you come to us with a presentation that gives primacy to a forecast on the intimate life of mosquitoes, when your own manifest," Kilhn again held up the paper, "clearly states there are reports concerning the langer. Given the langer's unique position of being one of two red-blooded mortal creatures in the Creation Grid, you'd think they'd be given a rank above the mosquito."

"And fornicating mosquitoes at that," said Sore from beneath the table.

"Right you are Assemblier Sore. Fornicating mosquitoes."

"It's filth! I tell you. Filth!" added Lovely from the floor, raising a robed arm for emphasis.

Kilhn resumed, "Let me underscore a point for your consideration. Not only do you rank the mosquito above the langer, but you've neglected to include citations for your sources. One might conclude that you're suppressing evidence, though I'm guessing it's more likely a case of poor editorial skills. How can we have faith in the text without faith in its editor?

"In a moment, the interview will be continued by one of my colleagues, and then we can explore more closely the temerarious impulse to include your own commentary on the value of said reports. With my remaining time, I wonder if you might explicate the logic behind your extraordinary system of taxonomy, whereby the mosquito is the king of all elemental beings."

Kilhn made an offhanded gesture for Hig to proceed.

"Your Eminence, thank you for the generous observations regarding my work. I have much yet to learn. You are rightly impatient for an explanation, and I recognize the time constraint, but I must begin with a digression. 'The Shifting Breeding Zones of the Gray-Winged Mosquito' appears in abridged form as an appendix of *Inverting the Stationary Residue of Decay: Predictions* and *Recommendations for Implementation Suitable for the Lineal Descendant as the Author of Public Policy and Welfare*. Selection of the text by the Bureau of Root-Race Affairs and Security suggests its relevance beyond our narrow discussion and the confines of these walls. Unfortunately, the text remains the only recorded predictive work concerning the super-lower beings. And as the title suggests, its focus is limited to the gray-winged mosquito.

"With the generous sponsorship of Grand Archivist Hurley, my colleagues and I made an exhaustive search of existing histories and forecasts to isolate passages concerning super-lower beings. Several hundred archive boxes yielded a pathetic dearth of material, out of which a mere twenty documents were germane to the research parameters. Once we eliminated those under two hundred words, in accordance with the rules of this committee, twelve remained, all of which concern the langer.

"Since Rooters possess attributes setting them apart from other mortals, it is not insignificant, as Assemblier Kilhn earlier indicated, that Rooters and langers share the distinction of being the *only* warm-blooded beings inside the Grid. Where one lives in welfare blocs; the other lives *in the wild*. Thus inclusion of the langer is integral to a comprehensive study of the lower beings, particularly as they are a sort of cross-over or link between Rooters on one hand and the super-lower beings on the other.

"At the risk of twice offending you, I must reiterate that the extant predictive material concerning the langer is largely inaccurate and/or irrelevant to a history of the lower beings. In our overview, which you'll find in the top folder inside the presentation box, we've identified two modes of inaccuracy: temporal fallacies and genetic fallacies. That is, predictions that contradict events as they actually transpired, and claims that contradict an innate and documented fact about the species, in this case, the six known species of langer. In accordance to Assembly protocols, genetic fallacies are weighted over temporal fallacies, though I must stress, all material regarding the langer contains both fallacies.

"The brevity of the examples is also a factor, as we found no discussion of the langer in excess of five hundred words, with the majority just over the two hundred word minimum. While not strictly an issue of accuracy, the shortness of the examples does weaken their statistical robustness. The following examples will suffice to illustrate the problem."

Hig began a recital of the texts from memory.

"The first example is from the seminal work by Assemblier Kilhn, *An Encounter with the Elements: One hundred Years of Natural Phenomena Inside the Creation Grid*, which, as we are all familiar, correctly predicts a solar eclipse, two lunar eclipses, and a colossal sinkhole in the Fifth Circle. Typically such a work would not contain a discussion of mortal creatures; thus, Assemblier Kilhn's inclusion of the langer is understandably less persuasive than the work overall. I for one would be in favor of excluding this example from our survey, but I ask you to hold off judgment until I've recited the passage:

"'During the Age of Tyranny, the langer learns to fly by observing mosquitoes. A public health crisis develops as thousands of spotted langers, flying over the highly populated inner Circles, drop their feces on innocent pedestrians.'"

From behind the table on the floor, Lovely exclaimed, "Let the langers fly!"

"Shut up you dumb cluck," hissed Kone.

Hig resumed, "The next two examples are excerpts from long fragments without attribution:

"'The Lineal Descendant decides to live amongst the langers and employs a great many Masons to move the Palace into the Fifth Circle Langer Preserve.'

"'Langers are domesticated and brought into the homes of Rooters and Malkings.'

"The next example was composed some five hundred years ago. *Understanding the Risks of Not Aging* is the third and final volume of Assemblier Hain's popular predictive history on healthcare leading up to our current era.

"'When excavation for the first Malking-only mental asylum finally resumes, a new species of langer is discovered. These *burrowing langers*—as they will be named by the project's chief engineer—are blind and demonstrate no interest in living above ground.'"

A groan issued from one of the seated Assembliers. Others appeared to be slumping inside their robes. Hig pressed on.

"We conclude with a passage from Assemblier Kone's predictive analysis of religious experience amongst Malkings in the upcoming century. While I recognize quoting a text yet unpublished may be unfair and certainly demonstrates poor editorial practice, the choice to do so reflects both the paucity of material and the degree to which I personally urge the Honorable Assemblier to reconsider including the following in the final version of the predictive analysis:

"'The members of a fringe Masonic group, the Rite of the First Sorrow, are possessed with prophetic visions that unlock many secrets of the *Archaic Record*. They attribute their visions to having incorporated small quantities of the animal's [the langer's] brain into their own. As long as no langers are hurt in the process, the practice is not illegal, but the Masons themselves testify it is repulsive.'"

Hig surveyed the table of hushed Assembliers. "It's obvious I've misspoken again. I can only surmise that you disagree with my opinion regarding the exclusion of the langer material. Certainly, as you are the authors, it would be impudent of me to take such liberties with your work. We shall spare nothing for the compendium."

"The compendium?" asked Branch.

"Under Archivist Hurley's supervision and encouragement, we've begun a work to be titled *The Compendium on Lower Beings*, which shall be published as a supplemental to *Predictive Histories, Past Assessments of the Future, a Survey.*"

"Master Hig, we commend you on taking such initiative," said Branch. "However, as you suggest, the current material is clearly too scanty for a compendium fitting of the subject. Given the obvious rigor with which you've executed the task, I am of the mind—with enormous regret, I might add—that perhaps such a project is premature. It may be incumbent on us to set a quota of forecasts and predictive histories pertaining solely to the lower beings. In this way, the project might be picked up again in, say, a thousand years? By then you should be comfortably in place here at the Assembly and would certainly be an eligible Team Leader. Perhaps my colleagues agree?"

The question was met with emphatic nods by those seated at the table. Sore was now face-forward on the floor, a rivulet of drool wending its way across the linoleum tile towards Lovely now squatting in the corner methodically shredding the manifest into confetti-thin strips.

Hig's careful posturing risked exposure by a valence amplified by excitement and relief.

"Your Eminence, may I offer an alternative?"

"Speak freely, Hig."

"Given the existing deficit of material, rather than waiting until future preditions are current, we might compose a *retroactive* history based on data already gathered by the other sciences."

"Empirical data?!" Exclaimed Kilhn.

"You're suggesting reversing the course of history," added Kone. "Now you really have stepped beyond your station!"

Lovely had constructed a rather complex sculpture from the paper strips, laying them flat on the floor, one-by-one, each slightly curved, until the paper—once a single sheet of standard ditto paper—bridged Sore's rivulet of drool and formed a nearly perfect circle extending half-way across the room.

7

Gaps & Fissures

i

A Retroactive History

*P*redictive History & Past Assessments of the Future, Including Gaps & Fissures, New Methodologies & a Preliminary Look Backwards: A Survey. This upcoming text will provide students a measure of how robust the predictive sciences have become and their increasing role in our ongoing understanding of the future. Primarily a re-review of past achievements, the book also ventures into an emerging field, what many are now calling *retroactive history*.

As work on the survey progressed towards publication, Hig began a new project titled *A Retroactive History of the Langer*, all the while thinking about a similar approach to the Ninth Root-Race. Writing about the past meant one must do so without predictions or forecasts. It also meant the results were nearly impossible to verify without falling into the tautological trap of working towards known outcomes from the present or the future. The strength of the new method was its simplicity. To write about the past one simply looked at the past—however small the aperture or foggy the lens. The introduction of empirical data seemed counterintuitive at first, but Hig remained certain retroactive history would lead to greater accountability, besides forcing the Assembly to become less insular, as they would have to cultivate a rapport with other disciplines to obtain empirical data. The retroactive method had enormous corrective powers as well. A venture into the uncharted territory of the past would ultimately lead to a better understanding of the present. Its effectiveness mattered little, though, if the Assembly had no means to critique itself.

In the early days of the Assembly, the Kosmocratores provided self-contained research models and a rudimentary predictive methodology. From these early exercises, the Assembliers identified a number of predictive tendencies. Later, after the departure of the Kosmocratores, each tendency was translated into a probability, capable of quantifying with some accuracy a prediction's likelihood of success. The demand for wider applications and greater precision led to a set of algorithms designed to tame the many stochastic forces that determined the normal course of events. The results were staggering, and soon the public became reliant on the Assembly to provide structure and cohesion to the Grid. The First Assembly became the de facto guardians of the algorithms and increased energy was directed towards protecting the methods of prediction. Eventually, most predictive work fell to second and third generation Assembliers.

The derivations of the algorithms were called the *protoarché*, and a sociopolitical hierarchy developed within the Assembly based on the degree of access to them. For example, First Assembliers were also called *First Degree Protoarché*. Beyond the First, access was not always determined by generation, though *stations* did conform more broadly to *degrees*. An Assemblier was always a higher degree than an Analyst, who was higher than an Archivist, and all were higher than an intern. No one but the First Degree Protoarché knew the complete derivation of the algorithms.

Amongst Assembliers, it was common knowledge that the protoarché could be reverse-engineered; however, they were equally familiar with the consequences of doing so. The Malking-only mental asylum discussed in Assemblier Hain's predictive history of healthcare was primarily a storage facility for those who had defied the First Assembly, the Circle of Nine, and other heads of the bureaucratic elite. The asylum also housed extreme social deviants who had been determined to be unresponsive to ordinary incarceration. According to the sensibilities of the time, the worst of these were suicides. The taboo against suicide was grounded in a fear that it might actually work, that some suicidal Malking might find the key to disabling immortality. By point of comparison, Malkings cited the lack of such a taboo amongst Rooters, to which Rooters responded that a similar prohibition would exist if the totalizing degradation of living in welfare blocs without citizenship didn't make suicide a justifiable alternative.

Sociologists said Malkings had institutionalized mechanisms for coping with immortality. Ironically, these often mimicked Rooter mechanisms for coping with mortality. Malkings ordered their immortal existence into one hundred year spans, roughly the length of a Rooter lifespan. During each span, a Malking was expected to fulfill one career-path, including the cultivation of private interests and friends, as well as making a meaningful contribution to society. Following the end of one career-path, a Malking migrated to another. This might involve attending the University or a trade school, with the option of petitioning to remain on the earlier path for up to five spans. In such cases, Malkings were encouraged to disrupt the primary path with a secondary path for at least one span before continuing, the exception being First-level bureaucrats who remained in the same positions forever.

The census had shown conclusively that career-path trajectories were not, on the whole, upwardly mobile. Early on, a tremendous effort was made to move citizens outside the *High Discomfort Zone*, where the amenities were few and/or advancement was limited (careers were often generalized as being either *inside* or *outside* the Zone). High Discomfort Zones varied widely as did the time required to advance beyond them.

Since all Malkings were the same age, census data offered a particularly compelling view of their demographic. Although, given the plurality of career-path strategies and the absence of any significant trend of upward mobility, analysts refrained from generalizing the population as a whole. High Discomfort Zones proved the exception as debate on the topic was more extreme and vocal.

One popular precept claimed all Malkings would eventually exist outside High Discomfort Zones. Clinical psychiatrists argued that those remaining *inside* do so not by choice but because they are victims of *Hegemonic Distress Syndrome*. According to the *Manual of Immortal Statistical Diagnostics*, one out of three Malkings suffered from HDS, a number not inconsistent with the estimated fifteen to thirty percent of the population considered *chronic insiders*. Three existential preconditions known as *remote fault-line indicators* were used to diagnose HDS: rfl.1., dominance is not within personal control; rfl.2., dominance is not desirable; rfl.3., dominance is not deserved. Researchers were quick to add, however, that identifying the outward signs of HDS was nearly impossible. The assumption followed that whereas the *implicit* profile was simple because the hegemonic condition was universal and unchanging, the *explicit* profile was diverse and complex because modes of resistance varied by individual, causing greater conformity in some and deviant behavior in others. Many of these terms were introduced during the University's first critical debate on immortality, *Living Forever Well*, and have been used ever since across many disciplines.

Authors who disagreed that the High Discomfort Zones would one day be devoid of occupants accepted the validity of the three fault-line indicators but drew a different set of conclusions from the data. Instead, they argued, the FLI alone explained why so many remained inside High Discomfort Zones. Giving FLI universal primacy made the terms more robust. All Malkings were bound by the FLI; it was their presentation that varied. Or one could say, either everyone has HDS or no one has HDS. Malkings diagnosed with HDS were simply equipped with the most literal and self-conscious relationship to the FLI. Most would never experience such a *living* relationship. In fact, appearance could suggest just the opposite. Assumptions of entitlement and superiority, expressions of bigotry, and acts of violence were all possible outward indicators of FLI.

One study looked at the Malking conception of mental wellness versus criminal reform. Presented with a choice between the Asylum and the Prison, a Malking always chose the Prison, indicating a stigma against the only institution that provided help for those with mental illness. Critics responded that a prison term was rarely more than five spans. Moreover, a life term was considered a legitimate career-path and could give an applicant the edge over others with less diverse experience. Whereas the term of commitment in the asylum was more open-ended without providing any advantage to those lucky enough to be released. The designation

Until Defeat on a Malking's annual psycheval meant residency inside the Asylum for the duration of eternity or until the authority lost the power to hold the patient, whichever came first.

Problems with the Assembly's internal organization and its methods of analysis had accrued over the millennia, leaving a system out of sync with itself and the rest of the Grid. Examining the archival material related to the survey project, Hig had unearthed patterns of neglect and abuse. By following a single *prediction strand* from inception to the most recent point of termination (also known as the *prediction boundary* amongst those outside the Assembly, particularly when the scope was broader and less linear), Hig isolated instances in which a prediction had been adjusted to match real events; a real event had been adjusted to match a prediction; or a bad prediction had been allowed to stand despite little or no substantial correspondence with empirical data. Surprisingly, all three, alone or in tandem, had a low *synthesis threshold*. That is, if a prediction was contradicted by actual events and the prediction was not corrected, the events often corrected themselves in line with the prediction. Assembliers called this phenomena *predictive kerf*.

The fact that events and predictions were manipulated, that predictions were used to leverage events to conform with other predictions, that influence was used to affect policy and pave the way for a prediction's success (or *unpredicted advantage*), that Assembliers developed predictions from other forecasts, and that predictions rather than empirical data were used, multiple levels of distortion by compounding error had corrupted the Assembly's ability to produce reliable predictions.

Hig believed the flaws of the Assembly were systemic, and the Assembliers had produced the best possible results with the tools provided them. The methodology had originated with the Kosmocratores, which begged the question, *Why would they have created a flawed set of tools?*

The Assembly was built upon a primary mandate by the Kosmocratores before the creation of the First Root-Race. However, a second mandate followed, suspending the activities of the first. The primary mandate was then reinstated just before the creation of Ninth Root-Race, some five thousand years later, a date that marked the beginning of history. The biggest lacunae in the Assembliers' project concerned the period between the formation of the Assembly and the creation of the Ninth Root-Race. No official forecasts or predictions were made during the prorogation of the primary mandate.

Originally, nine members composed the First Assembly. Now there were eight. The missing Assemblier, Assemblier Nole, had defied the second mandate and was forced to resign after composing a predictive history of the first eight Root-Races. Unlike later disgraced second-generation bureaucrats who were demoted, institutionalized, or banished outside the Grid, there was no evidence of Nole's existence after leaving the Assembliers. While no one claimed to have read Nole's work, surveys indicated most believed it existed.

Hig had set about to find Nole's text. The Assembly archives were an obvious place to start, since interns were granted full access. However, their very accessibility made the archives an unlikely location for the simple reason that if the text was there, someone would have found it by now. Surely, Hurley, the one most likely to know, would have dropped a hint. If the text *had* survived, the Circle of Nine would possess a copy in their archives, but they were stricter than even the Assembly with regards to granting research passes. If just one copy of Nole's history existed, it would be housed in the Palace, but no one besides the blind cleaners were allowed entrance. Nor was the LD likely to make the Palace Library public. Maybe a petition? Or a blind courier? The Library of the *Archaic Record* remained the last option, but given its inscrutable indexing system, one might as well wish to die.

The Library housed the *Archaic Record*, broken into four books, totalling more than one million volumes, as well as the *Marginalia*, partly composed by the Kosmocratores as last minute addenda, with the work of Malking scholars accounting for the rest—totalling some forty million volumes and growing.

To locate an ancient text, one must first decipher the Creators' system of indexing. No approach had yet been successful. Many scholars had not only tried but were prideful enough to reorder entire wings of the Library just to demonstrate the robustness of their interpretive apparatus, even further complicating the task for subsequent researchers.

Hig thought this daft. If the Creators used a cipher to catalog the AR, the AR should remain in place, undisturbed, and the interpretive apparatus should move. Hig questioned why these dressed-up librarians were moving books around when they could be focused on how and why the books were ordered the way they were in the first place?

Recently, a union journeyman named Bison snuck into the Library during broad daylight—a task to be admired in and of itself, as union journeymen were never given research passes—and reordered a single stack, not according to any numerical system or even by subject but by a volume's cover and binding, following the dominance of certain materials and construction styles used during each era. For example,

Bison distinguished between the pre- and post-ascension use of pounded langer hide covers and langer gut spine thread. Bison, through some customized application of animal forensics, identified the predominant species of langer used in each era. The subtlety of the approach became particularly apparent with books manufactured immediately after the ascension when vellum came from the gray and Numan's langer, while gut string came exclusively from the penny-eating langer.

A less radical version of the system had been employed by AR scholars for eons, usually to verify authenticity or to establish precedence within a small group of examples. The failure to translate the practice into an indexing system could only be explained by the utter lack of imagination within the lead towers of academe.

Though Bison had reordered a mere single stack, Hig was confident the method could be applied to the entire Library. Regrettably, it and its subsequent applications were deemed illegal since Bison lacked sufficient 'Library access authority'. Briefly entertaining the notion of defying the sanction to locate Nole's text, Hig had spent a week wandering through the Library during early hours when the halls were mostly empty. Professor Frame was usually there as well counting seeds, a leather seed pouch empty on the table, the mortal Frame extrapolating each tabulation outward to its statistical significance. Walking through the maze of the AR, Hig sensed the ghosts of past claims on the future, and came to believe The Library of the *Archaic Record* would never allow a present claim on the past.

ii

Nole

"I'm running out of time."
—Assemblier Nole's last memo

Once Hig had exhausted the options to recover Nole's work, a deaf courier appeared with a single Rite Size archive box atop a creaking presentation cart.

The First Assembliers had worked from ready-made research models during the suspension of the first mandate. Assemblier Nole had, according to legend, composed a history *as the events occurred.* In doing so, the Assemblier apparently not only defied the second mandate but was in effect writing history before history had even begun. If true, Nole's exercise was the only example of *nonpredictive prehistory.* Even with Nole's work, the question of *what happened to the Ninth Assemblier* might never be answered. In the original charter, a copy of which hung in the Assembly cafeteria as a series of framed decoupages, the First Assembly was referred to as the Assembly of Nine, despite the fact there were only eight: Kone, Lamb, Branch, Kilhn, Cleave, Sore, Hain, and Lovely. The anomaly survived as Assembly patois to indicate the hopelessness of finding something—*It's in the Ninth Assemblier's file cabinet*—or to chide someone about the possible consequences of an ill-conceived plan—*They'll make you the Ninth Assemblier for that one.*

A single file lay inside the archive box. It was Nole's. The sudden development smacked of Hurley, and once more Hig was humbled to have such a mentor. *Speculations on Creation's Aftermath* concerned the events during and immediately following the fateful moment of Kosmocratores' departure. It was barely a page in length, including a seemingly incongruous footnote. The evidently unfinished work, composed of a short preface, a single speculation, and a title that indicated so much more, had little practical application save as a resource for comparative prediction studies. While the prose was awkward and naive, it did adhere to the three principal goals of modern prediction: *Accuracy*, *Relevance*, and *Depth*.

Speculations on Creation's Aftermath by Assemblier Nole

Society grows yet remains inside the circular wall of the Creation Grid. The Malkings cannot die, cannot breed; our numbers are finite; our population is static. I tell you, our perfection can be felt by the stars! Blessed be the Kosmocratores!

The Root-Races remain mortal; they breed; their numbers increase, generation by generation, necessitating aggressive vertical development and recurring quashing. At large, the population is not prone to think about the world above or beyond the walls, what's called the Surroundings. Some venture out and make accounts. Most agree about its inhospitableness. But historic circumstance care nothing about temperament or disposition! And in the end, historic circumstance will force them to speculate about the world beyond the walls!

First Speculation: The Departure of the Creators.

The Kosmocratores disappear. Some expect their return. Others doubt their existence. Most are happy simply knowing they can name their own Creators. And yet if anyone wonders—and they all do—*Where did they go? Where did our Creators go?* They might as well be asking, *What lies beyond the Grid? What lies out there in the Surroundings?* *

To know an event before it occurs one must take risks and reach for things without a mind for popularity or success. The truth relies on us to do so. This is how we wish things were. This is how we say it could be if we all stood along a straight line. But it is not so, and we don't stand together. And we can't take risks, and we cannot reach for things without a mind for popularity or success. And there is no truth if the truth is blocked by prohibitions that will make these very words a crime.

---

*To witness these abominations one must have a courage equal to that of the poor half-creatures bound by fate to endure both their own creation and their extermination.

Rather than proving or disproving the apocryphal stories, Nole's text made one wonder why censorship had been considered at all. Deviations from the conventions of modern prediction were certainly present, but a radical or inflammatory spirit? The predictive elements were mostly extrapolations from current events, interspersed with praise of the Creators. While using the predictive apparatus supplied by the Creators, Nole had crossed a line by reflecting on events already past, contradicting the *forward trajectory*, as required by the first and second mandates.

Any analysis of early prediction work had to address verb tense. For the first three thousand years after the ascendancy no protocol existed, and Assembliers used whatever tense pleased them, often heralding the one most recently learned. This changed after the publication of Assemblier Kohn's monumental, *Cursing in the Future Tense*, which thereafter set the predictors' tense standard. Exceptions persisted, most notably Assemblier Pilchard's predictive history charting the return of the Imperial Palace to the Admin District written entirely in the past perfect. With few exceptions, Nole wrote in the present tense.

The second and last document in the file was Nole's medical record, including a psycheval coinciding with the composition of *Speculations on Creation's Aftermath*. A page titled 'Recommendations' was otherwise blank apart from the phrase *Until Defeat* rubber-stamped in red ink, the handwritten initials AL beneath it.

Attached with a paperclip to the back of the psycheval was a note. Hig recognized the handwriting as Assemblier Lamb's:

"As per the vows we uphold and the obedience we've always shown, by the glory of the Kosmocratores and their volcanic ashes that color our bodies and mute our valences, we condemn the conflagrant influence, for a body burned can be burned no more. By violation of our second mandate, the heretofore Assemblier Nole will be known as Secretary Nole and shall leave the Building of the Assembliers for the Admin Building and the Bureau of Statistical Prediction and Numerical Consequence."

By moving the starting date of history forward, from the creation of the First Root-Race to the Ninth, some believed the Kosmocratores eluded the embarrassing catalog of errors left in the wake of the first eight Root-Races. Nole's footnote hinted at this: "...the poor half-creatures who must endure both their own creation and their extermination." One has to ask, then, whether Assemblier Nole was banished for violating the mandate or for a footnote that predicted mortal genocide.

A history based on prediction could never unveil the past, could never unveil the truth of the first eight Root-Races. Who were they? What happened to them? Do they still exist? No mere immortal could answer these questions. These were questions for the gods. At least Nole's text provided a credible answer as to why they had forced history in the wrong direction.

While sifting through early predictions in search of Nole's text, Hig was struck by the phrase "Nole's *Damned Addendum*," recurring in the work by Assembliers immediately following the ascension of the Creators. Without explication or other contextualization, the authors seemed to assume a shared understanding with their readers. Could the reference be anything other than Nole's footnote? If so, the Assembliers' familiarity with the text must be greater than they now indicated. A moot point in any case, but the possibility aroused Hig's curiosity, and certainly helped alleviate the tedium of reading such a vast quantity of material that yielded so little to the query at hand.

And then Hig found a predictive history by Assemblier Lovely concerning the transpotation of the Imperial palace —a surprise in and of itself as the Assemblier had produced nothing but gibberish for the last two thousand years. Stylistically it was similar to Hig's vision of a retroactive history. Indeed, the content revealed a number of inchoate retroactive tendencies as well. By employing *hindsight* to contrast Lovely's history to predictions concerning the same temporal block, Hig made a tally of respective accuracies and inaccuracies, then excerpted relevant passages for bracketed annotation.

To start, let me quickly summarize the forecasts relevant to the one at hand and provide my subject a context, which I hope will be useful. As per the Kosmocratores instructions, the Palace was built in the center of the Creation Grid, the Admin District around the Palace, and the nine circles around the Admin District. By the Kosmocratores' *First Mandate Regarding the Exact Position of the Lineal Descendant at All Times & the View Thereupon by the Servants of Their Lord*, the Lineal Descendant has absolute power of state but is forbidden from leaving the Palace. According to the same mandate, looking upon or being looked upon by the Lineal Descendant is forbidden by any subject, mortal or immortal. The Kosmocratores established the Circle of Nine as a liaison between the Palace and Admin District. The Circle of Nine also functions as the judiciary for the First through Eighth Circles. [All legal matters concerning the Ninth Circle are overseen by BRRAS, who employ their own law enforcement and judicial agencies. Both are considered the most underworked agencies in the Admin District.] They are to fulfill the Lineal Descendant's wishes by implementing them into the rule of law and ensuring that all civil and criminal issues are handled within the same purview. ...

[The exile of the Lineal Descendant transpired ten thousand years after the departure of the Kosmocratores.] The origin of Lineal Descendant's exile can be traced to a violation of the above mentioned *First Mandate Regarding the Exact Position of the Lineal Descendant at All Times & the View Thereupon by the Servants of Their Lord....* The Lineal Descendant's sudden embrace of domestic policy soon led to the declaration: "I will not suffer alone." [Initiating the Age of Tyranny.]

After an honorable attempt to implement the Sovereign's request, the Circle of Nine found themselves confronted with an insurmountable problem. As will be seen, the solution irrevocably alters the very foundations of the Creation Grid and its inhabitants. The Circle of Nine conspired against their Lord by terminating all communication with the Palace. The tactic severed the only link between the Lineal Descendant and the nerve center of the Grid, shifting power away from the Palace to the Admin Building. The Imperial response was to bellow, and this horrible sound could be heard as far as the Ninth Circle and, no doubt, beyond. Days and nights passed and still the bellowing unbellowed. [Anecdotal data does not support this claim.] The Circle of Nine agreed the Lineal Descendant must be sent into exile. Thus began the plan to transport the Palace beyond the Creation Grid wall.

A challenge of engineering, ethics, and law, the transportation was not a simple task. The brunt of the logistical support was borne by the Masons' Union. Because the Lineal Descendant could neither leave the Palace nor be seen by mortals and immortals alike, disassembly of the Palace was ruled out. During the early stages, the assumption reigned that the Mason's Union could provide the necessary labor. No one anticipated the reaction of even the most seasoned workers once they began hauling of the Palace and its mournful passenger. [In fact, events lead to a split within the Masons: those willing to haul and those not. The later stopped in protest, eventually changing the name of their lodge to the Rite of the First Sorrow. Indeed the distinction between those who would haul and those who would not presages the division between Operative versus Speculative Masons of which we are now accustomed.]

With some trepidation I shall relay what next will happen. [As self-respecting Malkings, we know gender and reproduction are devices managing the central problem of mortality. The absence of these elements in Malkings is not, as some mortals would have it, a lack, as there is no presence a priori.] Over half of the remaining Masons hauling the Lineal Descendant became afflicted with an agonizing fear that they were killing their father. When questioned on this point, none indicated confusion as to their fatherlessness. However, many claimed their emotional landscape presumed the existence of a father, despite knowing the idea to be false. [After the splinter group of Masons coalesced under the banner of the Rite of the First Sorrow, we see the first instances of pseudo-Root-Race behavior. The behavior arose from the Age of Tyranny.]

The Masons employed leverage and lifting devices, magic, and the sweat of ten thousand Malkings. Faced with the depletion of half their workforce, the Masons mounted pressure on the Circle of Nine to replace them with Root-Race mortals, arguing that the recent softening of the prohibition against mortals working by allowing their employment as domestics created ample precedent. Should the recent softening be read as a perversion to be curbed or an opportunity that deserved even greater softening? What dangers might too much softening bring? Further complicating the issue, the policy shift allowing mortals to work as domestics came about from pressure by the mortals themselves. Unfortunately, these same activists were not lining up to help haul the Lineal Descendant across the whole of the Creation Grid.

141

From this juncture, the obvious prediction path would anticipate resistance to further softening if mortals remained outspoken about working as domestics but not as haulers, for as Malkings are their guardians, mortal volition is not irrelevant. Recasting the play of these elements, I shifted the course of the prediction to include non-union, rank-and-file Malkings. To my surprise, they became a robust indicator that contradicted the most commonsensical inquiry strand, leading me to the following conclusion: According to a growing number of mid- to lower-level Malkings, the mortals' behavior was perceived as hypocrisy and cowardice. The sentiment became codified in simple slogans, such as *If you don't like it, get off the Creation Grid*. In the end, the Malkings turn out to be the real hypocrites, as virtually none came forward to help with the hauling.

The Circle of Nine, bowing to public pressure, moved to grant the temporary employment of Root-Race mortals. But once again, logistical needs, political demands, and theocratic mandates put the project in jeopardy. The Circle of Nine required a reference from the *Archaic Record* to enact any change of law. This, they felt, was of even greater importance now that policy was being determined by the whims of the general citizenry and not those of the Lineal Descendant.

Perhaps at this juncture, with change in the air and their Sovereign halfway to nowhere, they will recognize that isolating the Lineal Descendant left state policy vulnerable to the fickle hearts and minds of the lower echelons. We can only hope they are drawn back to the true wisdom of the Kosmocratores. According to my predictive data, it is more than likely they recognize their actions were brash and regretful. But with the Palace now dragged well into the second circle and a public up in arms about putting the mortals to work, not to mention the months of bellowing [see earlier note], they will probably conclude there is no choice but to proceed, if only to save face. [Lovely sticks to this assumption, one that proved entirely accurate.] …

At no other time was the study of the *Archaic Record* so alive as it was during the exile of the Lineal Descendant. In the planning days, scholars were given the task of culling scripture for clues about building machines capable of transporting the Palace across the Grid. Following, they were asked to find aids of magic. Finally, as the Palace reached into the third circle, and rank-in-file Malkings began expressing solidarity with the Operative Masons, scholars were called upon to find some precedent in the *Archaic Record* that would allow employing mortals for the remainder of the hauling.

And they did.

Two passages from the *Archaic Record* 'Book One: The Age of Creation' were enough to convince the Circle of Nine. The first had been used once before to employ mortals as domestics

1) "And the Guardians may claim the discovery and turn it towards the path of the seven threads."

2) "For some *the real* is simply *the strength*. But as old bodies with abnormal teachers demanded new phenomena, Imogravi created a *system of the real*, emphasizing the roles of management, inspection, and accountability.

"Law emerged to mediate the struggle between more and less, the struggle between two particles, one deviated and expanded, the other ordinary and compressed. More and less became an exact measure of the other. Reconciled, they formed absence, i.e., unity.

"The clearest purpose of Law is securing Unity.

"Later, long after Imogravi became nameless, Law gave rise to intelligent workers."

143

So the mortals began to work. As might be expected, their small size and weak spirit quickly revealed our physical and mental superiority. As the saying goes: *The tallest mortal is only as tall as the shortest Malking.* Masons were overheard to say mortals were deadweight, which isn't far from the truth. A mortal under duress is disease prone, and disease often means death. At the nadir of the exercise, more Malkings were removing corpses than hauling the Palace.

Eventually, the Palace came to within one hundred miles of the Fifth Circle's outer boundary. Fatigue and disease overwhelmed the mortals, communications became confused, and soft hands weakened until the ropes fell slack. The Palace slid off its timber runners, settling lopsided in the mud, where it would remain deep in the heart of the National Langer Preserve until fate decides otherwise. [The conclusion is on target, but Lovely (understandably) misses the last minute introduction of psychokinetic levitation.]

Hig believed the texts by Nole and Lovely would be valuable resources as the theoretical and historiographical components of Retroactive History gained focus. In turn, *A Retroactive History of the Langer* would provide a model with which to write a history on the Root-Races. Indeed, since empirical data could now play a more significant role, perhaps even greater than census data, expanding the means of gathering and documenting real-world events became paramount. To begin a study of the Root-Races would require retrohistorical data—presumably from earlier predictive histories augmented by the socio-scientific research stored in the University Archives, hitherto ignored by the Assembly. A third source, one never considered before, required ingenuity, political influence, and resolve—not the usual requisites or means of a junior archivist. Hig realized that the present was more important to the past than the future. Obviously, the present would catch up to the future, just as the present would become the past, but to document the past, one must first look to the past, then to the present in its becoming the past, and finally, to the future in its becoming the present. In this way, Hig came to the rule of the *Hierarchy of Empirical Data: Past, Present, Future.* The irony that most knowledge of the past was derived from previous predictions of the future would always be at play. The inescapable past from the future lay before and after any step taken inside the Grid. As a data source, the present might be gathered without the strain of predictive methodologies. But the move from an unproven theory to actual practice required a delicate maneuvering inside institutions unfamiliar with change on any scale. Hig would begin by leveraging the First Assembly to negotiate a deal with BRRAS. There must be some way to observe the Rooters in real time.

8

dorthea

i

a text never read

As transcribed by the Kosmocratores for the education of the immortal mortals, the *Archaic Record* is composed in the Golden Shroud, the primary mystery language—the voice of the Impersonal Deity—which cannot be spoken, written, or thought. The Impersonal Deity is known variously as the Anti-Imogravi, the Double Dragon, the Unexistent Author, and the Second Prime Mover, depending on the intent of the invocation, the constraints of the season, and the depth of Agonie felt by the knower. This god fashioned the seven-spoked wheel from debris cast by the destruction of the first growth exhibition. The wheel whirled for three hundred million years. In such time, the soft stone became hard and the hard plants soft. The visible came from the invisible; and the insects came from small lives. The Impersonal Deity created the Kosmocratores from the emptiness between things, and they, by their turn, created the Animal Kings and the seven orders of Tiny Angels, undying, without sex, without hunger. These races belonged unbiased to the material and nonmaterial planes, numbered -99 to ∞.

When a demand arose to distinguish between particles, air and water represented the primary aspect modalities;

collected and ordered, they fit inside clear tubes and slowly formed the basic two-sided molecular variants and standard deviations: first-last; up-down; north-south; life-death; peace-turmoil; open-closed. In time, non-binary asmods produced a more nuanced system by incorporating the transient forms of the same elements: steam, ice, liquid, gas, mortal and immortal breath, miasma, aether, pungent air, dilute substance, mud, and salt. Only much later did objects and phenomena within the asmod spectrum manifest as shallow surfaces and Agonie.

Animal Kings will always be immortal. The nine orders of Tiny Angels will always be the invisible symbols of the Impersonal Deity. Mortals will always know themselves to be mortal. Tiny Angels are known only to themselves. Animal Kings house all possible mortal flora and fauna. Mortals know nothing but the past.

Of the nine Root-Races—the first shapeless, the second skinless, the third boneless, the fourth blind, the fifth deaf, the sixth speechless, the seventh mindless, the eighth soulless—only the Ninth was wholly formed, only the Ninth had need of keeping. They are hairless and walk upright. They are gifted with language. They are born without knowledge. They must defecate and enjoy activities.

ii

carnival

Every year after touring the middle Circles, the annual Carnival of Creation came to the Ninth. Subsidies from BRRAS barely covered expenses, and while Rooters could buy merchandise, they had to do so with chits. The carnies, who considered their occupation a cash only business, knew the Ninth Circle would never be profitable. So it was every year. And yet they looked forward to entertaining the mortals. The thriving black market and back ally haunts offered a quality of experience unheard of within the Immortal Circles. Above all else, nothing beat a Rooter audience. Malkings' elemental limbic systems curtailed emotional excess, but not wanting to be outdone by the mortals, they perfected rehearsed displays of excitement, and though quite convincing, they were transparent to carnies versed in the arts of performance and deception.

Many carnies were drawn to their trade by a profound discomfort with the role of Guardian, and the stage show provided an outlet for deeply rooted masochistic tendencies. Hungry for entertainment and innocent escape, Rooters found nothing more rewarding than depictions of Malking misfortune *by* Malkings. Thus, the Ninth Circle became a stage where Malking performers could humiliate themselves before an audience wishing to see exactly that. The act featured simple, physical skits free of dialog, narrative, or moral urgency and included the bum kick, the beard pluck, the mocking circle, and the upside-down spin. The more brutal Malking-baiting acts like maiming, burning, the *poo poo show*, and tooth and nail torture took place after hours in the black market districts. The mutual reward of these performances engendered strong bonds between audience and performers, and the evenings ended in boisterous conversation, frottage, and a free flow of alcohol and narcotics.

The Ninth Circle tour included Rooter performers as well. Lemm Ulder and his younger brother El-D both lived in Dorthea's housing bloc, and you could find them nearly every day practicing their clown act in the quad between spires. At some point during her pregnancy with El-D, Melinda Ulder became fervently pro-Malking, an absolute anomaly amongst Rooters. Melinda could count herself the only Rooter in their sector—and probably the entire Ninth—who welcomed the blue light. Her apartment, which Dorthea had seen once while lobbying residents to boycott the annual meetings at the Welfare Stadium, was something to behold. Radiant blue flooded through the windows, drenching the living room, overwhelming all other colors. A polaroid collage of First Circle bureaucrats covered the wall directly across from the barrage of light. At the time, it made sense to Dorthea. Rooters had no religion, but if they did, she supposed it would look something like Ms. Ulder's apartment.

Today, Lemm and El-D had dressed up in the parodic likeness of Malkings. They wore long, beard wigs and short stilts with cloth taped around the bottoms like hoofs. Something shiny (perhaps clear nail polish) suggesting rheum encircled their eyes. They had fashioned a great proboscis from a piece of langer intestine stuffed with a sock. Encouraged by an enthusiastic audience, they continued off stage and paraded below the workers from the Root 9 Preserve who dutifully and unperturbedly worked on one of the security lights that surrounded the quad.

In Malking society, carnies were considered barely a step above gender affects and drug addicts, when, in truth, their high valences and a relatively wide emotional range meant a greater kinship to First Circle administrators. The difference came in the divergent application of these faculties. Where one used valences to secure power and status, the other used them to enhance performance and stage presence. For one, a developed limbic system enhanced the ability to analyze

Rooter psychology and interpret the *Archaic Record*. For the other, it enabled an intuitive grasp of humor and pathos.

As Lemm and El-D made a tour around the audience, Dorthea realized the utility workers weren't repairing anything; they were installing surveillance cameras around the perimeter of the housing bloc. As the carnival carried on, she heard others talking about the cameras, and not just from her bloc. Before the final Malking humiliation, she knew it was a circle-wide effort. The startling shift of policy would dominate the bloc meeting later that evening, but unless someone had concrete details, the discussion would be alarmist and counter-productive.

iii

After the carnival, before the bloc meeting

She leaned with a foot against the plexiglas train kiosk, documenting the utility crew's activity by notation and a few discreet photographs. Her parents' politics, their incarceration, and presumably, their death put her the shortlist of Ninth Circle radicals. She was probably born on that list. But given the Malking way of thinking, the designation actually gave her more leeway than someone without a record. Once BRRAS labeled her a subversive she became a known quantity; a box checked and filed under *solved: threat status zero.* She might get arrested for taking pictures in broad daylight, but once they'd processed her and determined her behavior fit within the parameters that tagged her a second generation radical with probable intent to destabilize the Creation Grid, they'd let her go.

151

Gale, whose parents weren't political, stood a higher chance of being incarcerated. As a threat to their predictive capacity, he would be sentenced to prison and/or a stint in the Asylum, accompanied by some form of cerebral augmentation. The friends who had survived the ordeal returned estranged from the world and appeared unfamiliar to those who knew them. Throughout the Ninth Circle, one could find homes for their care and rehabilitation. With few exceptions, those taken away came back sterile.

Dorthea believed her near-immunity to be a gift from her parents. By bombing the Imperial Palace, the most radical act on the books, an action without political gain, they understood it would give Dorthea a deeper cover by way of greater visibility, a virtual shield against detection, as the Malkings' protocol to keep predictions directionally correct usually trumped their will to rule by jurisprudence. This, she knew full well, testified to the influence of the Assembliers upon a population of immortals otherwise inclined to follow the legal scripture enforced by the Circle of Nine. The best chance she had of being arrested was to sign up for a baking class, and the most extreme expression of her immunity would be to commit a single act of terrorism with impunity. She believed this was her parents' ultimate intent. Many Rooters—and Malkings for that matter—misunderstood why the radical ideology inherited from her parents advocated acts of terrorism, assuming attacks against the immortals were meant to weaken their control, when in fact, Rooters were the intended audience of all subversive acts. Her father had said, "There is no rebellion until we all know rebellion is possible." Every action, even Lemm and El-D's clown act, showed a single possibility that flew in the face prohibition. The great failing of the movement had been its inability to communicate this distinction.

Malkings were vulnerable to their own assumptions. Desirable or undesirable, if an action confirmed an expectation, it was ignored. And not just the political. Rooters depended on this weakness every day. The black market, for instance, was a zone lacking in nearly all punitive consequence because it conformed to a Malking expectation about Rooters. However, no one understood *why* the Malkings behaved this way. Some believed it was symptomatic of an intrinsic amorality. Without a true sense of right and wrong, all actions were either inside or outside a prescribed set of options. Others argued that in a culture that gave primacy to forecasts, value was measured by predictability. A third argument, which Dorthea believed could contain the other two, held that the Malking ontological condition made morality impossible and degraded the capacity for action based on necessity. Further, immortality diminished the value of security, the need for safety, and the perception of danger. These explanations could account for the segregation of Rooters, as a 1) moral indifference coupled with a desire for convenience; 2) culture of prediction eliminating the variable of civil liberty; 3) systemic—and irrational— fear of the mortal other.

And yet, thought Dorthea, *none of this can account for why the Malkings are installing surveillance cameras around the Outer Ninth.*

Since Rooters were already segregated within the Welfare Circle, large-scale monitoring wasn't necessary; moreover, there was no precedent. She remembered a few isolated instances with specific targets, but nothing like this, nothing so general.

Segregation gave Rooters the strength of solidarity, which helped them develop intrinsic, trust-based means of communication. Segregation engendered a healthy skepticism of

Malkings and their social policies. Dorthea was certain integration would actually make things worse.

Change amongst Malkings, though extremely rare, nearly always had a destabilizing effect on Rooters, creating uncertainty or fear in some and overconfidence or indignation in others. The Ninth Circle existed in a state of flux, ever torn, ever mended, lost to the ways of living without choice.

The utility workers had spotted her for sure, and she hesitated. Her first fear reaction was to drop the camera in the culvert, but they just nodded; Dorthea made a short wave back, not really knowing what else to do. *Pathetic!*, she thought, and blushed.

Her near immunity caused a low-level resentment in the cell. Some entertained a perception she could never earn her place because she could never really fail. Her parent's hero status only made things worse. Yet they all recognized the enormous asset her status brought them and their cause. And much of her leadership position came from being able to do things the others couldn't without getting arrested.

She saw Gale across courtyard, cutting through the audience now dispersing, many still laughing or mimicking the performers as they walked towards the marketplace or back home, back inside the *glare*. The carnies broke down the stage, loading their gear into a trolley that would transport the show to the next housing sector. Gale carried a white paper bag. If only a plain bean cake, without filling, whatever he brought would be delicious just because he'd brought it.

"Are you *Malking* crazy!? This is not a good idea... You here... And them over there."

"My day was fine, how about yours?" He was wearing standard issue blue overalls and his checkered cap. She grabbed his shoulder and turned him about-face.

"Come on; let's walk."

"The meeting's about to start; we've gotta go the other way."

"Cripes."

They turned around and crossed the street towards the meeting hall. The roads were meant for bicycles and Malking utility and public safety vehicles. Automated electric trolleys circled around the Grid. They ran day and night, stopping a dozen times in every sector. Where the commercial storefronts in the other Circles sold goods and services, the storefronts in the Ninth offered a mix of community bicycle and appliance repair shops, food distribution posts, self-service water outlets, and a proliferation of bauble shops, which took chits earned by recycling, filling potholes, or giving simple repair demonstrations. Every block had at least one back room dedicated to black market commerce. Rooters selling to other Rooters; Malkings selling to Rooters; Malkings looking to hire Rooters who wanted to work; Malkings and Rooters looking for narcotics or sex. Whatever Rooters did but not in public, they did in these back rooms—a life inside a life, filling in the missing pieces. The Ninth Circle was even home to a few fallen Malkings.

Just blocks from the meeting hall, Gale said, "Oh, I forgot this," and handed her the white bag, while hopping on one leg to pull up his sock.

"Are you okay over there?"

"These crappy socks from the d-center by Emit's. I swear they're worse than ours."

She stopped as he braced himself against the rough metal exterior of a food-post. The haggard-looking Malking inside waved them off pointing to the wall clock. She lifted her white paper sack and pointed to it sarcastically.

"It's some kind of new material. They just drop to your ankles, plus they itch like—damn it all. I can handle itching or dropping but both is *too* much."

Dorthea opened the bag.

"Whoa! Where did you get this?" She said extracting a perfect turnover.

"You know that crazy Malking who wanders around the courtyard?"

"Yeah, your friend, Malcolmb the Malking."

"Not exactly my friend, but anyway, Malcolmb had a whole box of these."

"And what did you have to do for it? Is that why you were way over by Emit's?"

"You're way too cynical."

"No, I'm serious. Even with the nice ones: nothing's ever free."

"I had to cop dope."

"Malcolmb the Malking is a junkie? That's perfect. And now I love you even more. You've given me a wonderful... cherry?"

"Raspberry."

"Raspberry! Wow, cool, a raspberry turnover! So not only have you won my heart, you've helped push another Malking towards the edge."

She took a bite, her back against the storefront's plate glass window, and slid down to the sidewalk. Gale did likewise, then unlaced his boots, removed the offending socks, sand threw them towards the storm drain. She passed him the pastry.

"Man, that's really good," she said.

"Get this, they came from an Malking-only restaurant in the Third Circle."

"Do they even have taste buds?"

"Yeah, right."

"Why bother? I mean, what do they need with flavor?"

"Malcolmb said the trend is authenticity."

"As if they haven't taken enough already."

"It gets worse. This place is called The Rooterie."

"Here, take the rest; I'll tie your boots."

They continued sitting against the corrugated steel watching the light turn gray and blue.

9

Foment

i

Meeting #1

Would community meetings exist if the Malkings hadn't introduced them over a thousand years ago? They had, so rather than being a testament of Rooters' strength in the face of adversity, meetings were one more instance of the Malkings' institutionalizing empowerment before it emerged on its own. Most Rooters believed the meetings had been reclaimed and were now divorced from their origin. A vocal minority believed otherwise. Regardless of their position, nearly all Rooters attended the meetings and complied with the original rules of procedure.

The community meeting system was structured as a hierarchy of consensus. It started at the most basic bloc-level. The Blue Spires were grouped into housing blocs sometimes called compounds; these, in turn, formed districts, districts formed sectors, and nine sectors made up the Ninth Circle. Bloc-level meetings were forums on local issues open to anyone in the same housing bloc. Issues with wider import were brought by elected representatives, called Extralocals, to district-wide meetings. Similarly, districts were represented by Superlocals at sector-wide meetings. Finally, three

159

representatives from each of the nine sectors formed the One-Twenty-Sevens, who convened the Circle-wide meeting, held annually or when special circumstance demanded. Each year the annual meeting convened at one of the nine sector welfare stadiums and was open to the public. Unlike lower meetings, One-Twenty-Sevens had a potluck atmosphere and little was accomplished beyond a review of the year with a positive look forward. Closing comments ranged from staid pablum to outraged incitement. Ask any two Rooters why the annual meetings culminated so frivolously, and you would get two different answers. One would say the pressing issues had already been resolved, and the year-end meeting let everyone come together on their own accord. The other would say the public nature of the Circle-wide meetings risked being infiltrated by Malking informants so a show was put on to mollify their suspicions that Rooters were anything but bauble-wearing nitwits.

Dorthea believed both explanations omitted two important factors. First, a Circle-wide could never achieve true consensus. Second, Rooter's lacked any influence beyond the Ninth. No meeting would lead to wresting power from the immortals anytime soon. In fact, large-scale resistance might lead to punishment but would more likely provoke no response at all. And as counterintuitive as it may sound, nothing was worse than something.

Following these assumptions, Dorthea focused on local politics, where true consensus was not only possible but could lead to direct action. Staying true to the path of her parents, she directed her effort *for* Rooters rather than *against* Malkings.

Much of what was known about Malking motives and intents came from sympathetic professors and students at the

University plus fringe elements of the trade unions. Using their own improvised methods, they gathered some intelligence themselves. Any given data pool was subjected to axioms developed during the Age Tyranny: Establish a true negative for a true positive. That is, with each supposition first demonstrate its fallacy, then, if that fails, demonstrate its veracity.

Dorthea and Gale approached the meeting hall. Bendt, the guest speaker, paced in front of the door. They'd never met, and what she knew about him came from the meeting announcement and the gazette. She'd figured with all the cameras going up, he'd probably be speaking on the subject of surveillance.

"Bendt? Yeah, I'm Dorthea; this is Gale."

Gale shook Bendt's hand, probably holding it longer than necessary. Bendt did not make eye contact. He looked the part of someone who spent too much time indoors alone, grinding through numerical representations of life. Gale discreetly wiping a hand against the back pocket of his overalls confirmed her guess that Bendt's palms were sweaty. He didn't shake Dorthea's hand, but only because she didn't offer.

Bendt had just moved back to the Welfare Circle after graduating from the University. He'd been born two buildings down from Dorthea and Gale's. His parents were *slave-claimed* when he was five, and he'd spent most of his childhood helping them run the household of their sponsor, a bauble merchant with an apartment in the Third Circle. After the Age of Reform and the end of *slave-claiming*, Bendt became eligible for college and could subsequently remain outside the Ninth indefinitely.

Rooters returning from outside had to put up with an improvised vetting process by their peers. It was always prudent to assume a prodigal child had been compromised.

161

Bendt wished to change this perception as quickly as possible. Returning was unusual but not unheard of, and there's no doubt leaving behind parents and life as a freed-Rooter would be difficult for anyone.

At the University, he studied statistical analysis and prediction. During his final year, he began exploring how the tools he'd learned could be used to help Rooters in the Ninth. At the University, they made predictions using models, so every result could be compared to a closed set of possibilities. Apart from old census reports, little data existed with which to formulate predictions about the Ninth Circle.

As the three entered the meeting, Dorthea tapped Bendt's arm and handed him the polaroids taken earlier; then she and Gale claimed two of the last seats towards the front of the room.

Bendt retreated to the back and ran the pictures through a hand-held magnifier, nodding and shaking his head. He quickly scribbled a few predictive equations to incorporate the new data, then furtively engaged a tangle of analog extension cords and adapters.

The five Extralocals sat at a long table facing the room. Elaine, an Extralocal and the Meeting Administrator, unpacked a metal bell wrapped in tissue paper and placed it on the bell-cradle already assembled in the middle of the table. As the Meeting Administrator, she was in charge of giving and taking the floor, the first being indicated by pointing at the person to speak, the second by a striking of the bell.

As Bendt remained intent on his AV equipment, and Elaine stared straight on gripping her bell stick, the attendees began a murmuring that quickly grew into a mad squabbling regarding the sudden influx of Root Preserve utility workers.

Elaine struck the bell. She began, "Ladies and gentleman... Ladies... Gentleman..." The five Extralocals beside her raised and lowered their arms to subdue the attendees. Then a voice rose above the clamor, "You Malking Anus!" Looking back, they saw Lemm and El-D wrestling in the foyer.

The room became otherwise quiet. Elaine did not strike her bell. And together they waited for the boys to finish

Elaine resumed, "Tonight we have a guest speaker, a speaker who may address some of your concerns. A son of our own bloc. Bendt Luld from a freed family. He was born and spent his childhood right here in the Forty-Fifth. Recently he graduated from the University with a degree in statistics?"

"Statistical Analysis and Prediction."

"Statistical Analysis and Prediction. At the very least we'll learn what that is. Um, okay, I'm sure we're all looking forward to hearing Mr. Luld's story."

The reaction was a mix of quiet reservation and open support.

Elaine gestured to Bendt who stood awkwardly. Extracting himself from the wires, he retrieved poster board charts and tables from several places in the room.

Walking to the front to face the group, he began.

"Given this is a community meeting, there's no doubt what's on your minds, so I'll jump right in with an analysis of the surveillance cameras with regards to their sudden appearance and a preliminary theory about why they might be there. The analysis will create two useful opportunities. Most immediately and with little effort, we can determine the Admin's intentions, or rather, we can eliminate many obvious possibilities. Secondly, we can use the data to create the first-ever predictive model created for and by Rooters. Dr. Frame,

163

with whom I studied at the University, is an obvious pioneer, but as we know, has chosen to serve the side that will not die.

"Oh, and speaking of this—sidebar here—I was thinking we might use the motto 'Rooters fight for the freedom to die!'

"Anyway, with regards to the first, we can assume that unless another Age of Tyranny is on the horizon, the cameras will probably not affect our lives. That is, they do not pose a threat, not a threat directly to us. If you review the records of our existence, the Lineal Descendant is the only one who has ever enacted any kind of repressive action. I believe he is, based on outdated intelligence and a survey of past behavior, in a remorse phase. Obviously, this does not explain what, if anything, the cameras are actually *doing*.

"A slight digression. At the University, our predictive work was based on data already modelled. Some of which concerned the Lineal Descendant. Blind to how such material might be valuable to us, the Academic Data Distribution Center gave our group two models to replicate: a predictive work leading up to the LD's suicidal ideation and a step-by-step prediction projecting the formation of a dust mote. I just thought that was kind of amusing."

Dorthea wondered if Bendt genuinely considered the remark a footnote or if it had been included to gain attention.

An almost tearful voice from the back of the room cut through the clamor all asking the same thing: "Is it true?"

"Excuse me."

"Is the Lineal Descendant suicidal?"

By the emotional tone of the question, Dorthea knew it was Melinda Ulder. The dead giveaway, though, was the eye-rolling voice from the foyer, "Ah, Ma."

"There's good news and bad news regarding the LD. The work I've done indicates with some surety that our *mother-father* in the Palace is quite suicidal. Problem being the immortality factor. Given the improbability that suicidal ideation will in fact become suicide in all the ways we mortals enjoy, it promises a return to the days of tyranny, which forces me to rephrase my initial claim: There is no good news regarding the LD's suicidal ideation."

Melinda Ulder quietly got up and left the meeting room. Her children said nothing.

"Right. Okay, let's talk about surveillance. By my calculations it appears highly improbable the video data is being analyzed or even viewed for that matter." I have a visual aid here—" Then the chart and tables drawn on smooth poster board slipped though sweaty fingers. Dorthea came to his aid, but by the time she'd rescued the props, and they were securely in his hands, the meeting had moved on without them. Elaine rang the bell, and announced, "Given the volatility of today's topics, we've determined postponing the meeting until next week is in the best interest of the group. The meeting is adjourned."

The attendees made a slow movement towards the door, and thirty minutes later, the room was clear of everyone but Dorthea, Gale, and the two Ulders, Lemm and El-D. Bendt approached, obviously confused. "Why did they stop the meeting? I barely got past my initial comments."

"The committee hates upsetting topics," said Dorthea.

"What else are there…?"

"Exactly," said Dorthea.

"We'd like to hear more about your work," said Gale.

Bendt made a minimal acknowledgment of their solicitation.

165

"It's why we came to the meeting," said Dorthea.

"The cameras," said Lemm.

Now Bendt looked up, making eye contact with Dorthea alone.

"You moved here pretty recently, right?" She asked.

"I was born here." Which sounded defensive.

"I get it," said Dorthea. "People think you're a fink because you came back from outside."

"It's understandable," said Bendt

"Maybe so," said Dorthea. "But you're still back home."

"I'm just a bit tired of blanket generalities."

"This is my home, and I plan on staying here forever," said Dorthea.

"It won't be *forever*," said Gale.

"That's a good one," said Bendt. "One of the documents we had access to was an old census of the Ninth Circle. There are nine hundred and thirty housing blocs in the NE Sector with an average of two thousand occupants per bloc. Multiply that by eight, and you get roughly seven to ten thousand housing blocs in the entire circle. In any case, with that many things to watch, not even the Malkings could keep track of it all. I'm fairly certain the threat posed by the cameras is psychological."

"You mean they're not really cameras?" El-D asked.

"Shut up you Malking anus," replied Lemm.

"They may not be functioning cameras," continued Bendt. El-D elbowed Lemm.

"On the other hand they may be completely operational. For all intents and purposes, it doesn't matter. Once I knew roughly the number of housing blocs, I set about estimating the number of cameras within a five bloc perimeter and extrapolated a number for the whole circle. Calculating how many hours of video produced each day by all of the cameras in total; how many hours it would take to watch it, and how many Malkings it would take to staff such an enterprise—"

"That's like the joke, 'How many Malkings does it take to eat a bean cake?'" Said Lemm.

"—since the Malking population never changes, and their employment is always one hundred percent—"

"Tell'em. Tell'em the punch-line."

"One—"

"But it needs a Rooter to tell'em it tastes good."

"Bad. It needs a Rooter to tell'em it tastes *bad*."

"Whuh?"

"Bean cakes taste bad."

"In your opinion."

"—So the Malking population and their rate of employment can be used as constants. With what could be gleaned from the public record and the old census, I divided the population with the known jobs. Even in the most generous scenario—which doesn't take into account the shadow government within the Admin District, which, as we all know, is an industry unto itself—the remaining number of potential employees is nowhere near enough to handle even a third of the surveillance video."

Bendt presented specific scenarios built upon possible contingencies: Malkings could watch between fifteen and fifty video screens at once; they could watch video from select areas and/or times, where/when crime was highest; the cameras could be motion activated; they could be equipped with behavior filters; the Malkings could mentally scan the video; the video could be used in conjunction with telepathic monitoring, et cetera, et cetera. None, he said, would give them the means to review the video in a timely, meaningful way.

Dorthea was skeptical. She feared Bendt was focusing too much on surveillance without considering the possibility of raw data gathering for its own sake.

ii

Meeting #2

Telepathic surveillance was still a threat, something they'd been combating years before she was born. Currently, their single inside intelligence source, the same one they hoped would explain the cameras, was a sympathetic BRRAS official named Secretary Calf. The first documents arrived twenty years ago, pinned to the message board outside her parents' apartment. They provided enough background to develop a defense against telepathic surveillance. It became necessary reading for anyone operating underground.

Despite intelligence from covert sources, the fact remained, there had never been a confrontation from outside; assuming mind readers existed inside the Lead Hotel, no mortal thought or deed had elicited a response, not since her parents disappeared. Once again, Dorthea remained skeptical of the Malking's telepathy, even though she believed just as strongly that it was real. Malkings had no reason to care. What they did or didn't do with their power was arbitrary. After all, if you were immortal would you care about rebellion? Yet, if you were mortal, could you care about anything else? The thought made her sick.

Organized cognition, recognizable patterns, mapped topography, how-to directions, strategic planning, et cetera— these were the most vulnerable to interception by the Malking telepathic analysts, and yet Malkings had difficulty deciphering abstract thought. Thanks to Secretary Calf this was the weakness Rooters learned to exploit. They found that the unfamiliar and the needlessly complex lay the foundation of an effective defense. Vague conception, misunderstanding, confusion, the anxiety of forgetting or not knowing, even the anxiety of knowing became key components of the arsenal. Over the years numerous means of generation and deployment were developed and tested, but only a few were put into practice.

They coordinated a schedule with Calf to test prototypes. To establish a control response, they agreed on a set time read directions to an abandoned tunnel entrance. Calf then replied by telegraph from the BRRAS Data Analysis Laboratory. One full stop indicated *yes* (analysts had intercepted the transmission); two full stops indicated *no*. If the control was positive, the test went forward. If the control was negative the test was terminated to resume at the next appointed time.

Lug Nut earned his moniker after constructing the static-shield generator, which effectively blocked even the slightest thought pattern. While it was the most comprehensive and reliable means of defense, the device weighed over one hundred pounds, and the slightest motion rendered it inoperable. Several were now installed inside the tunnels, but it did little to protect those en route from the housing blocs. A method called *mirroring* became the standard defense. The practitioner recited coded path coordinates to a neutral location, while walking to the intended tunnel entrance. Dorthea preferred what was called *concrete diversion*, wherein one focused on an unrelated but equally concrete and linear thought pattern. By using path coordinates as a foil, mirroring risked attracting attention, but if executed correctly, concrete diversion ensured a neutral walk to the tunnel entrance. No blip on the radar.

Just as Bendt downplayed the threat of video surveillance, Calf had assured them Malkings capacity to record and decipher telepathic data was limited. The problem was twofold: 1) telepathy was a recent development and, as such, had yet to be fully developed; 2) only a handful of analysts at the Bureau showed a predisposition for the work. The Secretariat Committee had determined telepathy could not be taught, and having yet to find a key in the AR, analysts and secretaries— for want of a better explanation—resorted to metaphor: *It's like sitting in the dark or on a bike; it's like a pig in a poke; it's like two in the hand and one in the basket; it's like standing in a blind alleyway; it's like through an opening and out the other; it's like an eclipse in broad daylight; it's like lions in winter.*

iii

under Ground

Dissident groups had been meeting in tunnels beneath the housing blocs since the Age of Tyranny. New causes meant digging new tunnels or claiming those left behind. Meeting rooms were carved out between passageways; each with at least two exits leading to the surface and two false exits leading to decoy rooms or cul-de-sacs. Given the possibility of raids, tunnels were regularly collapsed, filled in and redug. Maintaining safety and security meant constant movement and secrecy. It meant groups were never formed lightly. Survival meant adhering to the tunnel protocol no matter what the exigent circumstances or personality issues. Every cell enjoyed autonomy but shared the responsibilities of security, upkeep, and development. An oversight board composed of one representative from each recognized group scheduled work duties and other crossover activities. The board assigned entrances, exits, usage times, travel routes to and from tunnels; it scheduled maintenance details and development projects for the entire community. Given the complexity of the work and the advantage of having a representative with the clout to negotiate for your cell, it was customary to elect senior members. A similar hierarchy extended to the relationship of cells to one another. When it came to meeting times and places, work details and the priority given one project over another, older groups had an edge. Younger groups called this the *toehold of the old guard*.

And despite their caution or because of it, no one knew which, there had never been a raid—not in Dorthea's lifetime—and no sign they were even in danger.

At dusk, Dorthea and Gale settled into concrete diversion mode. Until safely inside the tunnel, silence was the rule. To anyone concerned, they looked like a couple taking an evening stroll.

They walked across the quad past the housing compound into the building ruins along the Creation Grid wall. These had been abandoned for five hundred years, a vestige of the time before the blue spires. They entered through a gap in the cyclone fencing. In the background the familiar blue shown then evaporated, momentarily revealing the buildings hidden within. They moved along the familiar path.

...by comparing the results of these three studies, we can quantify the effect of media density on thought reception and projection...

...clearly, if there were monkeys, they would be close in kind with Rooter mortality. Professor Lemur has shown, through a close analysis of high-valence Malkings, that monkeys, if they existed, would share the same morphology as Rooters to within a grade of ten percentile points...

Dorthea and Gale passed a landfill, a cemetery, a playground, then entered the ruinous schoolhouse and walked in darkness down stairs to the boiler room. A steel plate covered with concrete bricks and a stack of pallets concealed an entrance to a loop-shaped pre-tunnel that routed them towards their housing bloc before returning to the ruins. The main tunnel ran directly below and was accessed through hatches buried at irregular intervals along the dirt floor. Tunnel protocol stipulated that no one used the same hatch twice in a row, thus minimizing the visible impact on the tunnel floor.

Once inside the tunnel proper, they confirmed that the static shields were activated before moving on towards the space of the Mortal Guard.

Once inside, Gale went to the copy room and mimeographed leaflets to be distributed at the next stadium gathering.

The Mortal Guard was no longer revolutionary, now more a cliché, symptomatic of something: A corrupt seniority system? No leadership or new ideas? Or a group fighting an enemy it didn't have to resist?

During Dorthea's great grandfather's lifetime, the fight coalesced around citizenship. Now, as the economy worsened and reforms trickled down from the Palace, citizenship seemed inevitable. Would greater liberty bring significant change to their day-to-day life? Dorthea thought not. Decrees from the Palace now favored phrases like *equal opportunity, inclusive community, working together,* and *changes in the coming days.* The first Blue Spires were being torn down, and a flurry of new construction had begun in the Seventh and Eighth Circles, home to industry and the freed-Rooters born in the Ninth. Rumors persisted that freed-Rooters were being hired in the Bauble district and civics courses were a requirement for children. For the first time Malking candidates were making appearances inside the welfare circle. Dorthea wondered if these changes had been even remotely influenced by the generations of mortal activism?

A new group, the Root Labor Movement, met down the tunnel. The RLM appeared more vital and, some argued, relevant. They sought the total repeal of mandates prohibiting mortals from working. *Employment for all mortals!* Many in the Spires responded enthusiastically. As the prohibition had originally come directly from the Creators, the RLM took their cause underground, away from possible recrimination and sanction.

Ever since the petition and formal appeal process became an effective way to gain freed-Rooter status, the Mortal Guard spent their time filling out petitions for the elderly and running off mimeographed handouts to get the word out. As a senior group, they managed tunnel maintenance, repairing the pits and the sinkholes and the cave-ins. These job used to be delegated to junior groups. Now things were all turned around. So many new groups had formed, most focused on single issues, like banning the term Rooter, removing the holograms, or creating a mortal-friendly calendar.

Meetings began when everyone was seated at the circular table. Dorthea had sponsored Bendt. He arrived, introduced himself to the others, then brushed off the dirt from the tunnels. Gale entered last, removing the printing smock, wiping the blue off his hands, and tossing the garment into the hamper. Dorthea had copies of the letter and passed them around. Gale was as surprised as anyone to see it and even more so to hear her divulge the origin of her name. They hadn't discussed including the others. She'd been beset by an unfamiliar resignation and wanted to rid herself of anything private.

"We cannot conclude anything with certainty, but the letter draws on my given name and the AR, suggesting a familiarity with both. What's not clear is what they want."

"Or more importantly, *who they are*," said Cal in the cryptic manner that annoyed Dorthea. And even her reaction nudged her a little closer to believing nothing they did or could do would ever reach Rooters *or* Malkings. They were all safe. No harm would visit them. Secret gatherings were meaningless. They were, in effect, *free*.

Bendt finished crunching numbers on the back of a *Petition for Citizenship flyer*, "The knowledge fields are dissimilar enough to significantly narrow the pool of probable sources (assuming there is only one) to approximately 0.00005% of the sentient population. The percentage being an estimate of those familiar with both the specific apocalyptic prophecy and Dorthea's birth name."

"So who then?" asked Layel. "Who are we talking about? Rooter or Malking?"

"If I can interrupt very briefly," Bendt said. "Sorry, but if you were to include our discussion as it has thus far transpired, my original calculation would be adjusted a fraction of a percentage higher, seemingly irrelevant, but given the small pool, likely statistically significant."

"What could you possibly be talking about?" asked Cal.

"Now that we all know; now that all of us here in this room know, et cetera, et cetera," explained Layel.

"But that's after the fact; there's no way that counts."

"Nothing in predictive sciences is after the fact, Cal."

"Layel's right. Nothing is after the fact," Bendt confirmed.

Augst had appeared asleep since the others arrived and spoke into folded arms, "If it's a Rooter, it's someone from the old Resistance; if it's a Malking, they're using some kind of hyper-refined predictive algorithm (you'd have to ask the new guy about that), or they're getting biographical information through a Rooter informant, which could be—and Dorthea believe me I'm not making a case for this but it's got to be ac-knowledged—that is, it could be either one of your parents. If I'm not mistaken, they were the only ones in the cell ever arrested. They were also the only ones we can say without reservation had both factors in common—"

Gale interrupted, unfolding his arms and scooting up closer to the table, "Dorthea and I talked about this and we both recognize the Ed and Candy scenario is a possibility. And *obviously* they have to be included in the pool. Obviously that's obvious. More likely, though, I mean in our conversa-tion we decided there's a better chance they told someone else in the cell. The type of thing that happens when people *trust* one another—"

Dorthea stopped Gale, a hand on his arm.

Augst continued, "Of course, if it is a Malking there might be an occult element like *fortified coincidence*—"

"He's right," said Bendt, reviewing a page-long series of calculations.

"Why am I always being interrupted?" asked Augst.

"Maybe because you're always asleep."

175

"How asleep could I possibly be, Cal?"

"Who's right?" asked Layel.

"Gale's right. Dead on right. There is a greater probability the leak came from a confidant of your parents than your parents themselves."

"That's exactly what we're saying, what Dorthea and I have been talking about all along."

"However," said Bendt. "With regards to our inquiry, whichever party told the Malkings is irrelevant. Either way it came from Dorthea's parents, which would actually be good in a way, since they'd be the point of origin. They named Dorthea, et cetera. Unfortunately, all emotion and fidelity aside, this is our best-case scenario. The other options are super bad."

Augst resumed, "Fortified coincidence, that's where this archaic form of predictive science originally created for the trade guilds incorporating the AR and a belief that nothing in the future can be foretold without serious input from an undisclosed pantheon of pre-Kosmocratorian gods, all of whom prioritize the unions' self-interest before all else. We know about the Rite of the First Sorrow, right? These guys make them look like a chunk of dried langer meat. They are way weirder and with almost total certainty located someplace off the Grid. Then there's telepathic data retrieval or some such, not your run-of-the-mill keyword telepathy. In this scenario they target a specific individual and monitor every thought, every level of every thought a mortal can think, nothing random and not just blurps or beeps, the whole bean twist—"

"The other day you said that was impossible."

Bendt raised his pen but didn't interrupt as Augst continued.

"They wouldn't even need an informant. But Cal's right, the normal jerk offs at BRRAS don't have this capacity. This kind of sophistication would be pretty high up the food chain. No Admin bureaucrat or investor has that kind of power."

"This is great," said Gale, "And we can all sleep more soundly at night, but these scenarios have a *who* but no *why*. In the end that's all that matters."

Augst sat up, rubbed his eyes, and resumed. "I can posit *whys*, but I assure you, the *who* is way more important than the *why*."

Bendt was doodling.

Layel said, "We need more than one person's input, and since Bendt is the only other person up to speed on this, let him get a word in edgewise."

Bendt looked around the table, then began a new set of calculations.

Augst continued. "The fringe union fanatics? Their interest? Their *why*? They probably want Dorthea as a mortal sacrifice. Her name being from the AR would be super intriguing to any Malking religious freak. Plus her parents were radicals, et cetera.

"The telepathy thing? The *why*? I'm guessing some Admin shadow agency we've never heard of was given the green light to advance the science of telepathy for the good of the Inner Circle."

"So our choices are a mortal we all know, a union Malking with a god complex living in the Surroundings, or a psychotic bureaucrat buried ten miles below the old Palace foundation. That leaves us just about where we were ten minutes ago," said Layel.

"So then what?" Cal asked.

"There's a fourth option," said Augst.

Bendt finished writing to the end of the page and said, "It could be the Lineal Descendant."

He surveyed the room then looked to Augst who gestured for him to continue.

"Since I obtained the predictive material regarding the LD's suicidal ideation, I've reconstructed the narrative using a number of analytic registers. The cross-register similarities have really strong predictive *tells*, which is unusual and strongly suggests they'd hold up to the Empirical Veracity Standard of Predictive Theory and Application—"

"This so cool," said Augst.

"Come on!" said Cal. "Since when do the bean heads run the meetings?"

"Since always," said Layel.

"The test was developed by Professors Grouse and Loris, also the authors of the LD suicide study. They're straight academics and have nothing to do with the Assembliers, *plus* they use these predictive tools to understand past and present social patterns by corroborating their findings with empirical data."

"Whoa," said Augst.

Dorthea said, "Can we please move on?"

"I tweaked their approach to be more sensitive to the history of an individual, the psychic profile rather than the broader social context they inhabit. The LD study was easy to work with since the social context is already very narrow. Anyway, I think I got some stuff Grouse and Loris missed. The LD is suicidal yet cannot die. But this does not prevent multiple suicide attempts. In fact, the attempts will escalate, becoming more and more death-like each time. Or less and less life-like. The LD has gender affect disorder as well. I can't tell what gender or if there's a gender preference sexually. I found no direct correlation between the suicide and the gender affect. The suicidal ideation is likely a response to twenty thousand years of isolation. The impossibility of death will at some point become impossible to deny. When the subject recognizes suicide is impossible the gender affect (a weaker neurosis predating suicidal ideation) becomes dominant. In the dominate mode, the *gender affect* develops into a full-blown *mortal affect*, something way beyond just sex and gender. Subsequently the subject tries with its every fiber to embody all that is mortal. When this stage concludes, the LD will seek a companion to make the perceived state of mortality more real. Someone to be mortal with. A wife or a husband or a concubine or something to enact the ultimate confirmation. Initially the move bears fruit, so to speak, without contradiction. Breaking the isolation goes a long way to confirm mortality. But any number of things can rupture the delusion, and these are set like a long line of interconnected snap traps. Two likely triggers: The relationship produces no progeny; or the companion dies while the LD does not.

"The belief in its mortality is now damaged but not broken, and the LD is again overtaken by suicidal ideation. Here the cycle will be shorter than before. The data I've generated suggests a dramatic escalation of suicide attempts, a complete elision of the dominate mortal stage (no wife, husband, or concubine), followed by a relentless reenactment of the Age of Tyranny—"

"Ok, I think we got it," said Dorthea.

Bendt resumed writing. Augst went to the kitchenette to heat water for an *Extreme Bean Tea*. Cal left the room to throw a ball against the tunnel wall. Layel didn't cry but looked like she expected to, then sat up abruptly and said, "Shit, shit, shit."

Dorthea and Gale remained seated, holding hands under the table, not speaking.

179

10

Toast

L ob halted work to, again, gaze at the toaster oven *Deluxe* sitting by the door. This had been going on for several long days. Lob's fidelity to work and duty had been lost to an intoxicating curiosity involving the object. *It is a wonder this Muse, this Curiosity, would visit upon an immortal with such force!* Locating a receptacle next to the battle grate (the purpose of which Lob had never been certain, only that every office had one), Lob plugged in the toaster and fiddled with knobs until the coils inside glowed red and the outside radiated heat. *Mortals make their intimacies by correspondence, communication, and commingling with objects. Can Malkings be taken by such things?* Lob lay down beside the appliance. From the floor, there was no distraction, no reports and requisitions and petitions and budgets and predictions or anything else designed to eat away one's days.

I shall extend my hand into the thing itself! What does it mean to counter misery? What does it mean to suffer? How can one being suffer and not another? How can one die and the other live? The most perplexing puzzles arose in the comparison between mortals and immortals! Where's the package or simple test? An evaluation? Instructions? Something that explained the options?

Lob's hand began to smoke. *Is this what it is to be mortal?* Remaining still to ensure the process wasn't interrupted, Lob was taken by fear. *How can a Malking know any likeness of*

181

the mortal? Did a hand in the toaster bring one closer to the other? Is this what they meant by a mortal affect? Fear became embarrassment. *Since no immortal is mortal, the conceit is irresponsible and lacks the character of a true protector; it is an insult to mortals as well.* Lob's hand was now on fire. The secretary remained dispassionate as heat overcame the solidity of the toaster and it collapsed half-molten. Unplugging the appliance, Lob watched the lead contract around palm, fingers and thumb, now a very part of the thing that had cooked it.

When Lob stood, the toaster followed. Several hard whaps against the desk did nothing but intensify Lob's anxiety about neighboring secretaries, their derision, formal complaints, and glee. *What kind of fool would they find? What kind of idiotic bumbler? And what about the LD? Would the crafty King or Queen of the Grid detect the encumbrance?* If not by the heightened powers of telepathy, then by the simple deduction that it was taking twice as long to find a requested report not on the docket. *But who could find a thing,* Lob wondered, *after the fateful day whence your hand becomes a toaster?!*

II

FOR THAT I COULD DIE (1)

i

MORTAL DREAM #1

Dorthea dreamt she and Gale travelled to a welfare stadium; they were late. They'd brought coins instead of chits, which meant going back to the first machine and starting over. The trolley was empty of passengers, but crawled with langers, hanging from every hand rail, congregating under every seat. Outside the stadium, banners were strung between wooden poles. They said *Welcome Mortals*. The stadium was empty. She rechecked the flyer. No date. *Mortals never die* scrawled on the inside page. They held hands, walking towards the bleachers. She counted steps. Losing count she began again, losing count, starting over, losing interest, walking without counting, walking to a side room beneath the bleachers.

A Malking stood in her path. Its body part water and spilling onto the floor. It put its arm around her. The arm was full and light. She yearned to collapse. The immortal held her close. She could see solid parts of it falling away to the water below. "I know you from afar," it said, then pushed her face against its stomach. She woke up nauseous, vomiting without waking Gale.

MORTAL Dream #2

On the border between the Grid and the Surroundings, Dorthea and Gale passed Malkings in orange overalls working from utility vans in caged lifts. Thick wires connected the Blue Zone to a power station on the other side of the Grid wall. They planned to sabotage the power station that fed the blue light in their sector. Built with rotary converters and mercury-arcs, a well-placed stick to interrupt the arcing would disable the the entire station. But finding the station had proven difficult. Outside the Grid the ability to discern, orient, and remember became compromised. The topography expanded outward from the wall with little variation, lacking markers that would help determine direction or distance, and they always got lost.

For the first half mile, trees grew in sand along a woodland trail, then the foliage and insects became sparse, and when the forest ended, the trail ended, and Dorthea and Gale were surrounded by sand, the furrows rising and cresting without visible end. Dry snow fell, accumulating on the dunes, then joining twisting eddies of sand, as the wind picked up, and they were hit from all sides by airborne sand and snow.

They both wore oversized orange jumpsuits lifted from the utility truck, taped off at the wrists and ankles, knitted face masks, and welding goggles.

She said, "It's just weather; we can make it. If we get lost, we'll find our way back and go again tomorrow."

So they forged the duststorm. Walking until first the wind and then the light receded. Now it was silent and dark.

The dark, silent place seemed steeped in fleeting odors, petroleum, floral, decay. Sometimes it smelled of untouched outdoor air. Uncertain if she was still breathing, Dorthea realized she was holding her breath, forgetting to exhale. She thought, *I witness their power, their graceless, over-earnest obedience to protocol.*

Small, round objects rolling across sheet metal; parchment paper unwrapping; low, brief laughter. Hammer blows and the cast-off of bone shard and hot blood. Now the smell of some killed thing. Draining blood turned into steady dripping. More voices, loud, too low to understand. Then cutting around the space she crouched. The ground simply broke away or fell or turned. Before her a Kosmocratore, smooth, featureless. Eyeless, mouthless. A flawless obelisk. Melting, the lead flowing into darkness. Dorthea floated in random orbit as the Kosmocratore went soft. A kind of light carried the other parts into darkness. She saw glimpses of foreign bodies from the past. The small authors, the seven-spoked wheel, the immortal rain. The image collapsed into ash. Imogravi wielding bands of steel. Plants and animals hid within undisclosed places. Some things like gods. Beautiful things. Things never wholly known. These things are ordinary because they have no difference. A chart formed of molten lead. It showed the generations of mortals: *first, second, third, fourth, fifth, sixth, seventh, eighth, ninth.* On the right-hand column checks marked their respective anatomies, psychic aspects, and vulnerabilities. Each is identical.

FOR THAT I COULD DIE (2)

i

AR, "FIRST APPENDIX: RULES OF FELLOWSHIP"

Vegetables distributed to Rooters shall conform to the specifications of size and shape determined to be the most appealing to Rooters—criteria derived from data gathered by survey. As the inner landscape of Rooters is not within the Guardians knowledge domain, predicting how vegetables should be presented requires careful analysis and execution.

Vegetables should be symmetrical and of a size that might be eaten at a single sitting. Exception: Occasional anomalies should be introduced so as not to aggravate the Rooters' fear of total order, a tertiary fear derived from their master fear. As randomness is difficult to replicate, the necessary algorithm has been provided in the next section. Anomalies should not stray too far from the norm. Simply changing the size (bigger or smaller) of a vegetable will have a pleasing effect and may even inspire wonder, as Rooters find solace in the unexpected. Similarly, that which is normally symmetrical can inspire a calming befuddlement when found to be asymmetrical. Thus, an extremely elongated mung bean, while unappetizing, will cause most Rooters not only to puzzle over its appearance but verbally share the encounter with other Rooters. A secondary benefit, then, is the power of the anomaly to forge kinship and passive unity. Conditions whereby you as shepherds of the flock (see "Appendix ii, Section c: Unexistent Animals") will learn to rule justly.

ii

Life only mocks this mortal desire

Dust. Dust forever. Following the failure of the guillotine, et cetera, I forged ahead: the arduous rendering into slurry, the desiccating and grinding into dust. Have you ever seen an automated mortar and pestle in full swing? Upon my word, I've been soaked, crumbled and blown, scattered to whatever extent possible, completely lost to the world of atoms and other small particles.

The psychic landscape of dust is complex. To be sure, my senses are less acute, and the overall condition of unity more amorphous. The invisible parts are still invisible, which continues to prove advantageous. One is without definite shape or volume. One is neither contracted nor expanded. In short, one is alone, but such an aloneness belies its earlier incarnation. With this aloneness no one feels sulky. Regarding the newest facet, being dust: I am transient and dispersed, dispersing as I speak, yet wholly without volition. Watch as I wade through crevasses, descend into pipes, escape with an upward swirl. I am migrated by wind, barometric pressure, cold and by heat, by rain, lightening and drought.

Freedom is being utterly without a head. Without a head, even the volition to protest the state of non-volition is foiled. Suicide may be an act of volition, but does my inability to conclude the suicide give me the right to claim I am anything but alive? And yet my headlessness does give me the right to declare I am free. When you learn that the lack of a head means the lack of volition, the lack of a head and the lack of volition become synonymous. The discovery of their sameness brought me to the last truth. Thus, in a state of dread and ecstasy, I end with the final lesson: freedom is lack.